P9-CDL-889

Tales *of the* Shimmering Sky

WILLIAMSON
TALES
ALIVE!

BOOKS BY SUSAN MILORD

ADVENTURES IN ART
Art & Craft Experiences for 7- to 14-Year-Olds

HANDS AROUND THE WORLD
*365 Creative Ways to Build Cultural Awareness
and Global Respect*

THE KIDS' NATURE BOOK
365 Indoor/Outdoor Activities and Experiences

TALES ALIVE!
Ten Multicultural Folktales with Activities

TALES OF THE SHIMMERING SKY
Ten Global Folktales with Activites

Tales of the Shimmering Sky

TEN GLOBAL FOLKTALES
WITH ACTIVITIES
RETOLD BY SUSAN MILORD

PLAINVIEW OLD BETHPAGE PUBLIC LIBRARY
999 OLD COUNTRY ROAD
PLAINVIEW, NY 11803

PAINTINGS BY
JoAnn E. Kitchel

A Williamson *Tales Alive!* Book

WILLIAMSON PUBLISHING
CHARLOTTE, VERMONT

Dedicated to the memory of Phil Currier, a stellar human being

Many thanks to all who contributed to this book. Special thanks go to Susan and Jack Williamson, for all their efforts to bring books and kids together; to Bill Jaspersohn, for his unerring editorial skills; to Joseph Lee, who wove all the elements of the book together visually; to JoAnn E. Kitchel, for the shimmering paintings that illuminate the tales; to Michael Kline, for his endearing activity illustrations; and to Mark Breen, who explained what goes on during a thunderstorm without taking away any of the mystery.

Copyright © 1996 by Susan Milord
All rights reserved.

No portion of this book may be reproduced—mechanically, electronically, or by any other means, including photocopying—without the express written permission of the publisher.

LIBRARY OF CONGRESS CATALOGING-IN-PUBLICATION DATA
Milord, Susan.
Tales of the shimmering sky: ten global folktales with activities /
as retold by Susan Milord; illustrations by JoAnn E. Kitchel
p. cm.
Includes index.
Summary: Presents folktales, background information, and activities related to beliefs of peoples around the world about heavenly bodies, the seasons, and the weather.
ISBN 1-885593-01-5 (alk. paper)
1. Astronomy—Folklore. 2. Weather—Folklore. 3. Folklore—Juvenile literature. 4. Tales. [1. Astronomy—Folklore. 2. Seasons—Folklore. 3. Weather—Folklore. 4. Folklore.]
I. Kitchel, JoAnn E., ill. II. Title.
GR620.M58 1996
398.23'6--dc20   95-47229
                              CIP
                              AC

Tales Alive! is a trademark of Williamson Publishing Company.

Design by Joseph Lee, JOSEPH LEE DESIGN
Paintings by JoAnn E. Kitchel
Activity illustrations by Michael P. Kline
Printing by Quebecor Printing, Inc.
Printed in Canada

WILLIAMSON PUBLISHING
P. O. Box 185
Charlotte, VT 05445
Telephone: (800) 234-8791
10 9 8 7 6 5 4 3 2 1

Notice: The information contained in this book is complete and accurate to the best of our knowledge. All recommendations and suggestions are made without any guarantees on the part of the author or Williamson Publishing. The author and publisher disclaim all liability incurred in connection with the use of this information.

Contents

Let the Sky Be Your Guide   8

Tales and Activities

The Division of Day and Night {CREEK, NATIVE AMERICA} 12

The Twelve Months {SLOVAKIA}   22

Let the Sky Be Your Guide

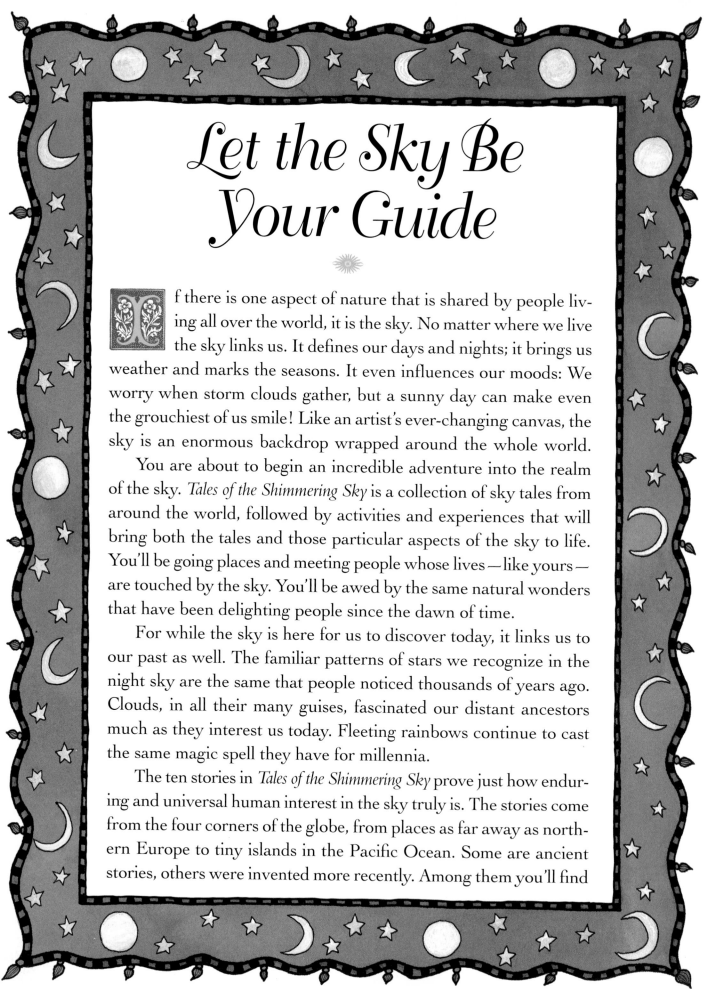

If there is one aspect of nature that is shared by people living all over the world, it is the sky. No matter where we live the sky links us. It defines our days and nights; it brings us weather and marks the seasons. It even influences our moods: We worry when storm clouds gather, but a sunny day can make even the grouchiest of us smile! Like an artist's ever-changing canvas, the sky is an enormous backdrop wrapped around the whole world.

You are about to begin an incredible adventure into the realm of the sky. *Tales of the Shimmering Sky* is a collection of sky tales from around the world, followed by activities and experiences that will bring both the tales and those particular aspects of the sky to life. You'll be going places and meeting people whose lives—like yours—are touched by the sky. You'll be awed by the same natural wonders that have been delighting people since the dawn of time.

For while the sky is here for us to discover today, it links us to our past as well. The familiar patterns of stars we recognize in the night sky are the same that people noticed thousands of years ago. Clouds, in all their many guises, fascinated our distant ancestors much as they interest us today. Fleeting rainbows continue to cast the same magic spell they have for millennia.

The ten stories in *Tales of the Shimmering Sky* prove just how enduring and universal human interest in the sky truly is. The stories come from the four corners of the globe, from places as far away as northern Europe to tiny islands in the Pacific Ocean. Some are ancient stories, others were invented more recently. Among them you'll find legends about the sun, the moon, and the stars, as well as unforgettable tales about wind, clouds, and rain.

Many of the stories in this collection offer explanations for the natural phenomena associated with the sky, from the markings of the moon to the crash and boom of thunder. The stories are colorful and creative, even fantastic. It would be a mistake, however, to judge our ancestors' understanding of the sky based on these tales. In fact, until recently, most ordinary people had a much keener awareness of the sky than we do today. For them, the sky was a clock, a calendar, even a map. It was, of course, also the inspiration for some wonderful stories.

After each tale in this collection, you'll find fascinating information about that particular aspect of the sky, as well as many things for you to do and make. There are experiments to help you understand such things as the reasons for the seasons and how clouds form. You'll find plenty of things to craft and to eat, many of which were inspired by beliefs about the sky from yet other cultures. For example, the first story, a tale about night and day told by the Creek Indians of the southeastern United States, is followed by a science project inspired by a Chinese legend, a yarn craft related to a sun tale told by another Native American people, and an outdoor game from the Philippines.

Throughout the book, you will be encouraged to go outdoors and simply observe the sky. Words cannot describe—nor is there any substitute for—experiencing the sunrise on a summer's morn, or spotting the barely-visible crescent moon hanging like a smile in the night sky. Being a skywatcher doesn't take any special equipment, and once you start really looking at the sky, noticing the beauty in all its moods, you'll be hooked!

So, let the sky be your guide. Come explore an aspect of our world that links all of humankind together—the ever-changing, ever-fascinating sky.

Bringing the Sky to Life

Each of the tales in the book is followed by a variety of activities. (If you need help, you shouldn't have any trouble persuading a curious adult to help you!) To fully enjoy the activities, keep the following in mind:

Before starting a project, read through the instructions from beginning to end. That way you'll know exactly what materials are needed and which steps (if any) may require an adult's help. You'll also have a better idea how long a project will take (most take less than half an hour; some may require longer for paint or paste to dry). Most projects have convenient stopping points, so you can leave your work and come back to it later.

The various projects require only everyday materials, so you should have no problem rounding up the necessary art supplies and cooking ingredients. Feel free to substitute similar materials (a slightly wider board or narrower rope, for instance; vanilla instead of lemon extract, and so on).

Be sure to get an adult's help when using a tool you may be unfamiliar with or not old enough to use on your own such as sharp knives and electrical appliances. The same is true when using a stove. Whenever an adult's help is required for an activity, you will be reminded to ask for it before going on to the next step.

Have fun!

A Word to Adults

Tales of the Shimmering Sky follows in the tradition of *Tales Alive!* (Williamson Publishing, 1995): It's a book written directly to and for children—with the hope that adults will accept an open invitation to join in the fun!

The stories and accompanying projects appeal to a wide range of ages and abilities. You can best judge a child's current interests and abilities, and offer any necessary help as needed. For example, children who do not yet read will still enjoy listening to the stories read aloud. Many of the projects, too, can be successfully completed by younger children, given a bit of encouragement and help from an adult.

One way you can offer invaluable help is by making outdoor observations possible. Do what you can to make such firsthand experiences enjoyable, from joining kids on the grass under the stars on summer nights to stepping outside after a rainstorm in search of rainbows. Sharing the wonders of the sky is certainly a great way children and adults can spend time together.

Finally, this is a book that can be used by larger groups of children, in such settings as schools, day-care centers, and clubs. Many of the topics lend themselves to group observation and discussion, and the hands-on activities can be adapted easily to larger groups.

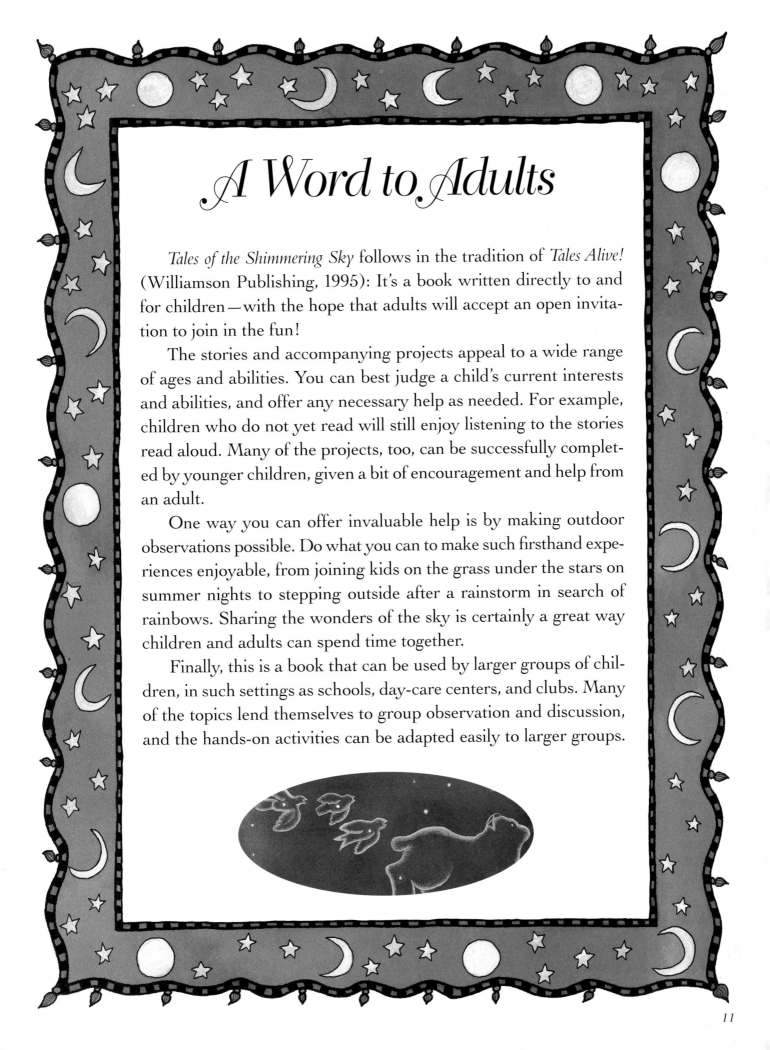

The Division of Day and Night

A Tale from the Creek Indians

Many Native American peoples describe the creation of the world as the time "when the animals could talk." Little wonder that this tale, told by the Creek Indians of the southeastern United States, puts the power of creating day and night in the hands of animals.

ong, long ago, when the earth was new, the animals were in charge of making day and night. The daytime animals used all their magic to keep the sun in the sky, so that it was often light for days at a time. Then the nighttime animals would triumph, and just as suddenly the sky would be pitch black for a week or two, or even more. And so it went, back and forth.

Not surprisingly, this created bad feelings between the animals who needed daylight and those who preferred the dark. The two groups worried, when conditions did not favor them, that they would have trouble building their homes and raising families. . . or that they might even starve from lack of food. Things got so bad that the animals called a meeting to find a solution to their dilemma.

The animals who preferred the daylight hours spoke first. As far as they were concerned, the sun could shine all the time. "That way," Bison said, "we will be able to graze whenever we're hungry, no matter what time of day."

Hawk nodded his agreement. "Daylight has my vote, too. I need the warmth of the sun to heat the air on which I float. And I need the light of day to build my nest and hunt for food."

3 1912 00293 2571

"Hear, hear," echoed Snake, who appreciated the way the sun warmed his body so that he could slither about. "There's nothing quite like a sunny day spent lying on the rocks. If you ask me, we could do without night altogether."

Other animals murmured their agreement, and a small cheer rose somewhere at the back; a few animals even began stamping their feet excitedly. With all the racket, no one noticed Owl silently gliding from the branch on which she was perched. She dropped down beside a small group of mice. Alarmed, they scurried for protection behind a wiry weasel.

Owl swiveled her head from side to side, gazing steadily at the animals that surrounded her. There were hushing sounds, then gradually the noise subsided, and all was quiet.

"That's all very well for you," Owl said, gesturing to the animals that had spoken first. "But I need the dark of night to do my hunting. For me, the daylight hours are totally useless."

A brave mouse stepped forward and, eyeing Owl nervously, said, "Owl is right. Night is best. Without the cover of darkness, my family and I would have no protection from. . . you know who." The other mice nodded their heads in agreement.

Bat waved his arms in exasperation and spoke. "Ever think what would happen to me if there were no night? I would starve, because the insects I eat only come out after sundown. Besides, daytime is for sleeping. Every bat knows that!"

Once again the air was filled with the sound of voices—angry voices and anxious voices, and those of animals who feared there might not be a peaceful solution to their problem. Who knows where this might have lead had Chipmunk not ventured to speak.

"Something just occurred to me," Chipmunk began. All heads turned in her direction. "I think Raccoon may have the answer to our problem."

The animals' attention turned to Raccoon, who looked startled by Chipmunk's pronouncement. He shrugged and shook his head. It was clear he hadn't a clue what Chipmunk was talking about.

Chipmunk motioned for Raccoon to turn and display his striped tail. "This is what I mean," the tiny creature said. "See how Raccoon's tail is divided into equal sections of light and dark? Why couldn't we divide day and night the same way—equally?"

None of the animals said anything for a moment. Then "Why not, indeed?" questioned Cottontail.

"Why didn't we think of that sooner?" exclaimed a group of squirrels.

And then and there, the animals agreed to divide each day in equal portions, so that the sun ruled the sky half of each day and the night reigned the other half. And so it is to this day.

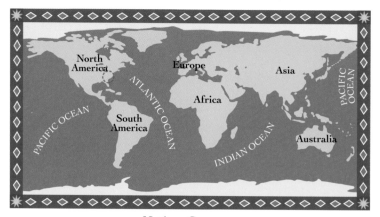

Nation: CREEK
Region: SOUTHEASTERN
UNITED STATES
Continent: NORTH AMERICA
Language: MUSKOGEAN

All Day Long

The sun is featured in many tales told around the world. As in "The Division of Day and Night," many of these stories illustrate our ancestors' concerns about day length—or the time when the sun is actually shining in the sky.

The Polynesians, people living in the region that stretches from the Hawaiian Islands to New Zealand, tell a tale about a time when days were much shorter. According to the story, the sun raced across the sky each day, barely giving the people on earth enough time to complete their chores before darkness came. The half-god Maui (rhymes with Howie) was so annoyed he decided to do something about it. He snared the sun in an enormous net made from braided coconut fiber, threatening to chop off its legs if it didn't slow down. So terrified was the sun that it agreed to slow its journey, a promise that it has kept to this day.

On the Move

Many ancient cultures regarded the sun as a powerful celestial being, one that traveled from one end of the sky to the other each day. Just how the sun made the journey was often related to popular means of transportation. The Vikings and Greeks, for instance, were certain the sun traveled in a wheeled chariot, much like the horse-drawn carts they themselves used. The Egyptians, accustomed to boating on the Nile, thought the sun sailed across the sky in a shallow boat. Other cultures believed the sun traveled on foot, while still others thought the sun had wings, soaring overhead like a slow-moving bird.

Star of Stars

Centaurus

What our distant ancestors did not realize is that our sun is actually a star, no different from the stars that are visible in the night sky. What distinguishes it from the tiny pinpoints of light we see on clear, dark nights is its proximity, or closeness, to the earth. The sun may seem distant at 93 million miles (150 million km) from earth, but the next closest stars, Proxima Centauri, Alpha Centauri, and Beta Centauri, a trio found in the constellation Centaurus (sen-TOR-us), are nearly 26 trillion miles (42 trillion km) away! For more on stars, see pages 60 to 83.

No Peeking! No Kidding!

CAUTION!

Never, ever look directly at the sun. Its strong light can quickly damage your eyes, causing permanent harm, or even blindness. This is true even during a complete solar eclipse, when much of the sun is hidden by the moon.

The Chinese have a tale that explains why looking at the sun hurts our eyes. As the story goes, two beautiful sisters once lived on the moon. While they sat embroidering delicate designs on silk, they were watched by the people on earth who were enchanted by their beauty. All this attention troubled the sisters and so they asked to trade places with their brother, who lived in the sun. "But even more people will see you, because the sun is visible during the day," he pointed out. The sisters had thought of that, and, to this day, they use their embroidery needles to prick the eyes of anyone attempting to gaze at them.

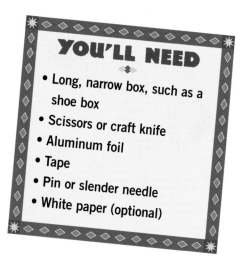

YOU'LL NEED

• Long, narrow box, such as a shoe box
• Scissors or craft knife
• Aluminum foil
• Tape
• Pin or slender needle
• White paper (optional)

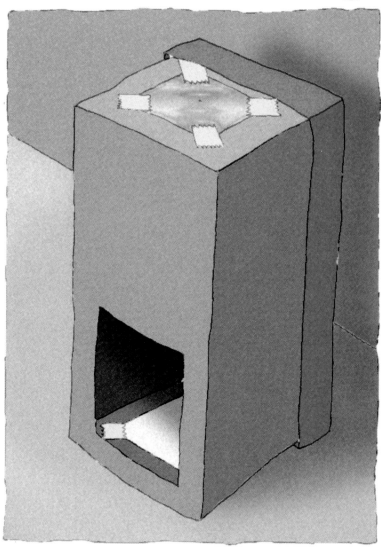

One safe way to view the sun is through a pinhole viewer. You can easily make your own. Here's how:

1. With an adult's help, cut a small, square opening at one end of the box. Tape a piece of aluminum foil over the hole. Prick a tiny hole in the center of the foil with the pin.

2. Cut a larger opening on one side at the opposite end of the box. If the inside of the box is a color other than white, tape a piece of white paper to the inside bottom of the box. (This helps make the projected image easier to see.)

3. Aim the pinhole in the direction of the sun, and look through the side opening to see a tiny image of the sun projected on the inside of the bottom end of the box.

EQUAL TIME

*The animals in the story agreed to divide day and night equally. You've probably noticed that, in fact, day and night are not usually the same length. During the winter months, for example, it may be dark when you get out of bed in the morning and dark once again before you even sit down to the dinner table. The opposite happens during the summer months, when the sun rises before you do and sets after your bedtime. It's only during the vernal equinox (or the first day of spring, on or about March 22) and the autumnal equinox (or the first day of autumn, on or about September 22), that the length of day and night are equal. You can remember this by recalling that **equinox** is Latin for "equal night."*

Me and My Shadow

We say the sun rises in the east each morning and sets in the west each evening but that's not what really happens at all. It's not the sun but the earth that moves. Every 24 hours the earth rotates from west to east on its axis, making objects in space appear to move from east to west.

You can demonstrate this apparent movement with a simple experiment on a sunny day. Stand on a paved area with your feet slightly apart, and have a friend trace around the outline of your shoes with chalk. Now have that person trace around the outline of your shadow. Mark your shadow with your initials and with the time of day. Trace around your friend's shoes and shadow in the same way.

Come back an hour or two later and stand on your shoe tracings. Trace around your shadows once again. What has happened to them?

Fun and Games

Children in the Philippines play an outdoor running game called Day and Night. A variation of Tag, this is one game you and your friends will agree is sun-sational!

You need an open space marked with boundary lines, such as a portion of a playing field or a soft-surfaced tennis court. You also need one flat shoe (a sandal or slip-on shoe works best). Divide players into two teams—one team representing Days, the other Nights. Have the Days stand at one end of the field, and the Nights at the other. Appoint one player from each team to serve as "shoe tosser."

The tosser from one team throws the shoe high in the air. When it lands, the teams run to opposite ends of the field. But here's the catch: everyone must wait to see how the shoe lands. If the shoe lands topside up, the Days attempt to tag as many Nights as they can before the Nights are "safe" at their new end of the field. Any tagged players become Days, joining the rest of the Days. If the shoe lands sole up, the Nights go after the Days, and the newly tagged Nights join their captors.

The game continues in this way—with the tossers from the two teams taking turns throwing the shoe—until the players end up either all Days or all Nights.

BEST OF TIMES

Even though we humans are daytime animals, many of us feel our best at certain times of day. Some of your family members may be raring to go first thing in the morning, while others claim they do their best work later in the day (or even well into the night). Which would you say you are—a day person or a night person?

Web of Wonder

YOU'LL NEED

- 3 slender, straight sticks, about 12 inches (30 cm) long
- Yarn or thick string, in assorted colors
- Scissors

The Cherokee Indians credit Grandmother Spider with bringing light to their world. According to one story, the sun was held captive by a greedy band of people who lived on the other side of the world. After several attempts to capture the sun ended in failure, Grandmother Spider offered to try. Carrying a bowl she'd made from clay, the tiny creature let out a single silken thread behind her so that she could find her way back home. She succeeded in stealing a tiny piece of the sun, and since that time, spiders have woven their webs in the shape of a circular, rayed sun.

Weave your own rayed sun design to hang as a wall decoration in honor of Grandmother Spider's daring deed. If you can't find any straight sticks outdoors, use chopsticks or a thin dowel sawn into three pieces.

1. Cross the three sticks at their mid-points, evenly spacing them. Wrap yarn diagonally around the sticks (changing direction every few wraps) to hold them together securely. Continue wrapping until a rounded yarn hump covers the sticks where they cross.

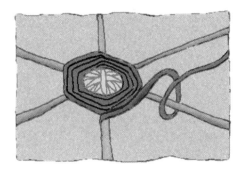

2. Using the same or a different color yarn (change colors by tying a length of new yarn to the old yarn, making sure the knot is hidden at the back of the work), begin the "weaving." Wrap the strand of yarn completely around one stick, then carry the yarn to the next stick, and wrap it completely around that one.

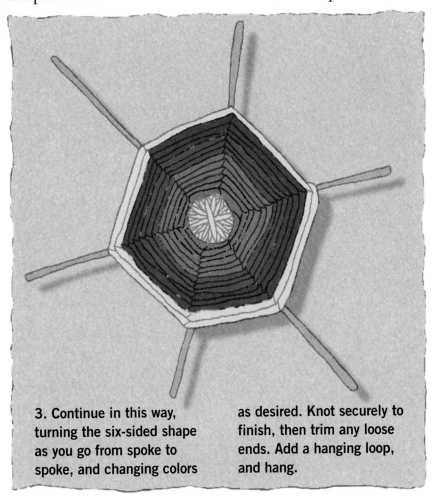

3. Continue in this way, turning the six-sided shape as you go from spoke to spoke, and changing colors as desired. Knot securely to finish, then trim any loose ends. Add a hanging loop, and hang.

The Twelve Months

❉

A Tale from Slovakia

The sun is also responsible for seasonal changes. As the earth makes its annual journey around the sun, winter is followed by spring, summer, and finally autumn; then the cycle begins once again. If there is any moral to this story from Slovakia, it's that the natural order of the seasons cannot be ignored.

High above a small village in the mountains, there once lived a girl named Marushka (mah-ROOSH-kah). Orphaned at a young age, Marushka had been taken in by a disagreeable woman named Mother Drozd (drohst) who had a daughter of her own—a lazy girl named Holena (hoh-LAY-nah). The two treated Marushka with disdain, but the girl did her best to forgive them their selfish ways, grateful as she was for the roof over her head.

It wasn't always easy, as Marushka shouldered more than her share of responsibilities and daily chores. While Holena and her mother spent most of their time daydreaming and complaining about their lot in life, Marushka cleaned the house, tended the farm animals, and cooked the meals. Happily, Marushka enjoyed keeping busy. Besides, she said to herself, when I'm in the barn and the garden, I don't have to listen to Mother Drozd's nagging.

One winter's evening, Mother Drozd and Holena sat idly at the dinner table while Marushka washed the dishes. The two began grumbling about the weather. The snow had been falling steadily all day, and Holena declared she was tired of winter. "I'm sick of all this white," she complained. "When is it going to end? I want to see green grass and spring flowers! I want to

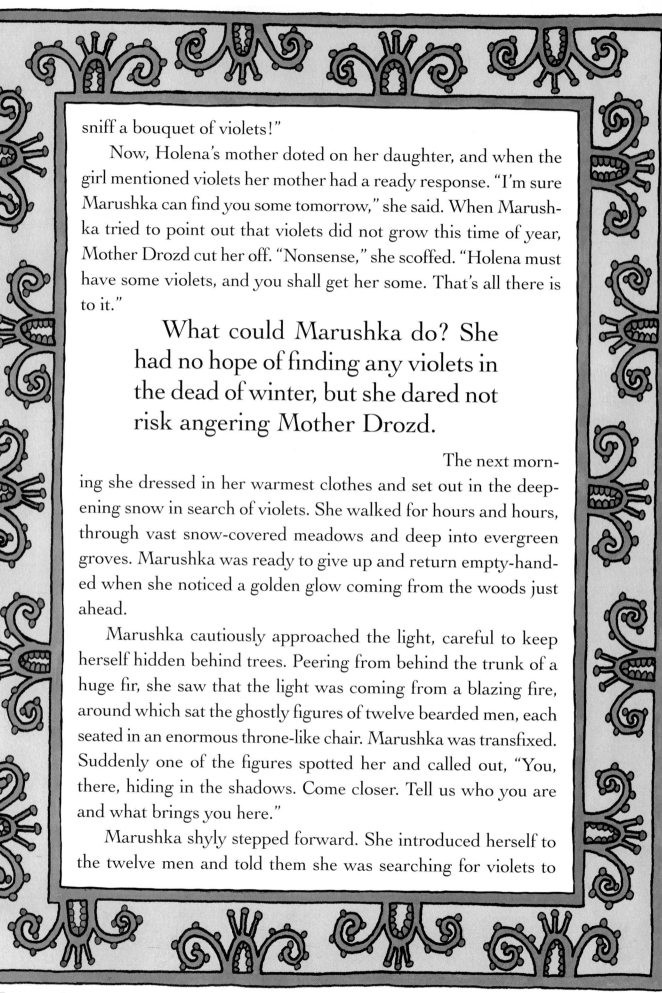

sniff a bouquet of violets!"

Now, Holena's mother doted on her daughter, and when the girl mentioned violets her mother had a ready response. "I'm sure Marushka can find you some tomorrow," she said. When Marushka tried to point out that violets did not grow this time of year, Mother Drozd cut her off. "Nonsense," she scoffed. "Holena must have some violets, and you shall get her some. That's all there is to it."

What could Marushka do? She had no hope of finding any violets in the dead of winter, but she dared not risk angering Mother Drozd.

The next morning she dressed in her warmest clothes and set out in the deepening snow in search of violets. She walked for hours and hours, through vast snow-covered meadows and deep into evergreen groves. Marushka was ready to give up and return empty-handed when she noticed a golden glow coming from the woods just ahead.

Marushka cautiously approached the light, careful to keep herself hidden behind trees. Peering from behind the trunk of a huge fir, she saw that the light was coming from a blazing fire, around which sat the ghostly figures of twelve bearded men, each seated in an enormous throne-like chair. Marushka was transfixed. Suddenly one of the figures spotted her and called out, "You, there, hiding in the shadows. Come closer. Tell us who you are and what brings you here."

Marushka shyly stepped forward. She introduced herself to the twelve men and told them she was searching for violets to bring back to Holena. The men listened in silence; then the one who had spoken first said, "I am called January. Surely you must know violets are not to be found this time of year."

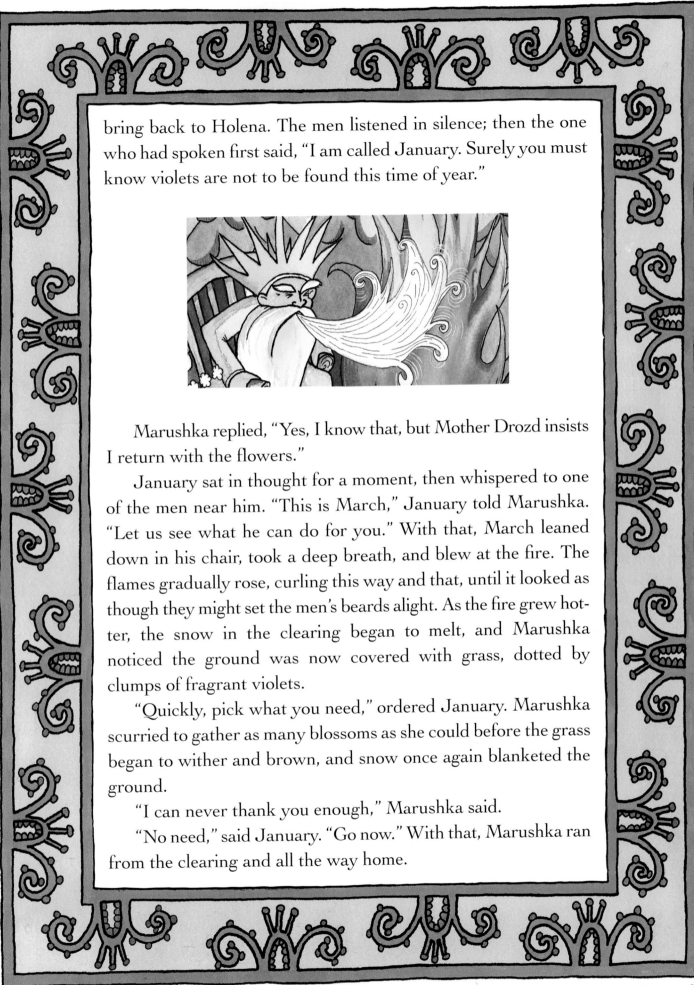

Marushka replied, "Yes, I know that, but Mother Drozd insists I return with the flowers."

January sat in thought for a moment, then whispered to one of the men near him. "This is March," January told Marushka. "Let us see what he can do for you." With that, March leaned down in his chair, took a deep breath, and blew at the fire. The flames gradually rose, curling this way and that, until it looked as though they might set the men's beards alight. As the fire grew hotter, the snow in the clearing began to melt, and Marushka noticed the ground was now covered with grass, dotted by clumps of fragrant violets.

"Quickly, pick what you need," ordered January. Marushka scurried to gather as many blossoms as she could before the grass began to wither and brown, and snow once again blanketed the ground.

"I can never thank you enough," Marushka said.

"No need," said January. "Go now." With that, Marushka ran from the clearing and all the way home.

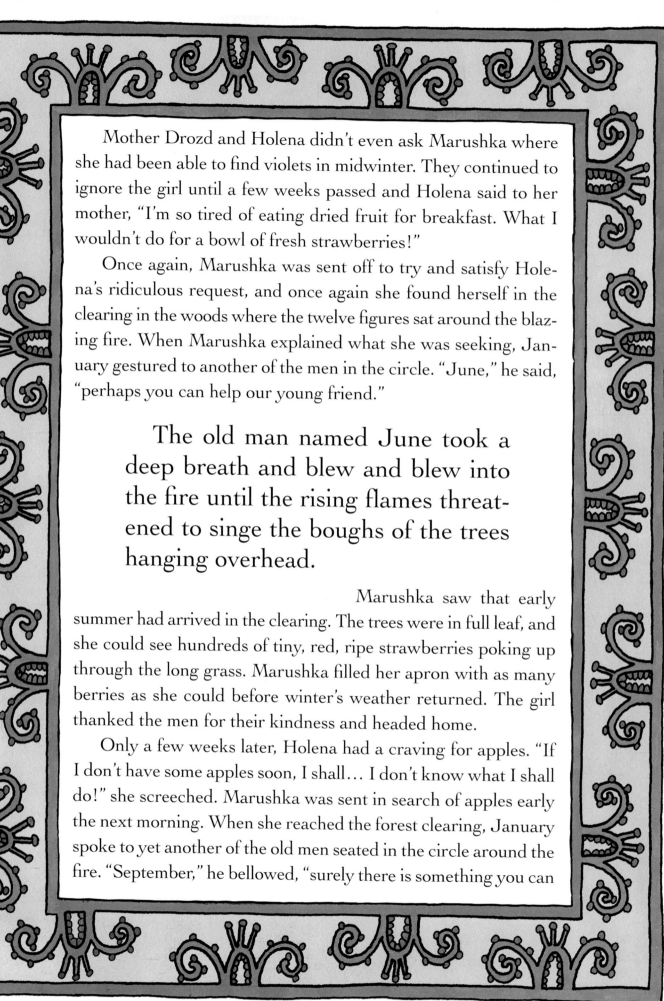

Mother Drozd and Holena didn't even ask Marushka where she had been able to find violets in midwinter. They continued to ignore the girl until a few weeks passed and Holena said to her mother, "I'm so tired of eating dried fruit for breakfast. What I wouldn't do for a bowl of fresh strawberries!"

Once again, Marushka was sent off to try and satisfy Holena's ridiculous request, and once again she found herself in the clearing in the woods where the twelve figures sat around the blazing fire. When Marushka explained what she was seeking, January gestured to another of the men in the circle. "June," he said, "perhaps you can help our young friend."

The old man named June took a deep breath and blew and blew into the fire until the rising flames threatened to singe the boughs of the trees hanging overhead.

Marushka saw that early summer had arrived in the clearing. The trees were in full leaf, and she could see hundreds of tiny, red, ripe strawberries poking up through the long grass. Marushka filled her apron with as many berries as she could before winter's weather returned. The girl thanked the men for their kindness and headed home.

Only a few weeks later, Holena had a craving for apples. "If I don't have some apples soon, I shall… I don't know what I shall do!" she screeched. Marushka was sent in search of apples early the next morning. When she reached the forest clearing, January spoke to yet another of the old men seated in the circle around the fire. "September," he bellowed, "surely there is something you can

do for our young friend." September looked doubtful, but he blew into the fire with all his might, sending the flames higher than Marushka thought possible. She watched in wonder as the clearing was transformed into a scene from early autumn.

Marushka ran to a tree that was laden with apples. She could not quite reach up high enough to pick the fruit but, thinking quickly, gave one of the branches a shake. Down fell a single rosy-skinned apple. Marushka took hold of another branch and shook it with all her might. Another apple gave way, but only minutes before the other fruit on the tree shriveled up and a fresh layer of snow covered its bare branches once again. Marushka thanked the old men for their help.

Holena and her mother were not impressed when Marushka returned. "What? Only two apples?" they grumbled. "Where are the rest? You ate them all on your way home, didn't you?"

Marushka tried to explain that she had been able to shake only two apples from the tree, but Holena didn't listen. She demanded to know just where the tree was located. "Useless girl," she snarled. " I see I'll have to go and get my own apples."

Holena bundled up in furs from head to toe. Even so, the spoiled girl was hardly prepared for the cold wind and deep snow. She was practically on her hands and knees when she reached the clearing in the woods. Holena barked at the twelve men, demanding to know where they kept the apples.

January was so enraged by the girl's rude behavior that he

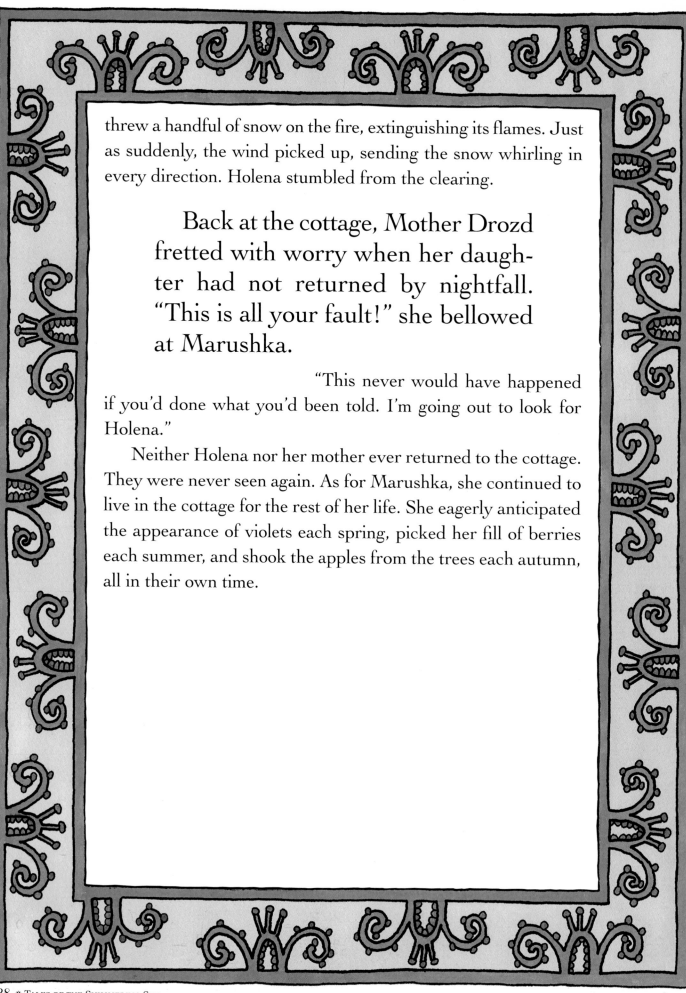

threw a handful of snow on the fire, extinguishing its flames. Just as suddenly, the wind picked up, sending the snow whirling in every direction. Holena stumbled from the clearing.

Back at the cottage, Mother Drozd fretted with worry when her daughter had not returned by nightfall. "This is all your fault!" she bellowed at Marushka.

"This never would have happened if you'd done what you'd been told. I'm going out to look for Holena."

Neither Holena nor her mother ever returned to the cottage. They were never seen again. As for Marushka, she continued to live in the cottage for the rest of her life. She eagerly anticipated the appearance of violets each spring, picked her fill of berries each summer, and shook the apples from the trees each autumn, all in their own time.

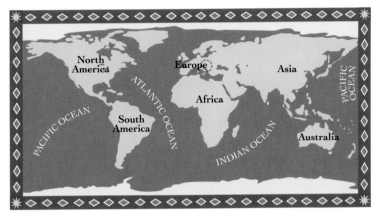

Country: SLOVAKIA
Capital: BRATISLAVA
Continent: EUROPE
Language: SLOVAK

The Fiery Sun

In "The Twelve Months," the roaring fire around which the twelve bearded men sit represents the sun. It's not hard to see the link between the sun and fire. Like the sun, a fire creates warmth and its flames are yellow. The Aborigines of Australia also describe the sun as a fire—one that is allowed to burn down each evening and is rekindled each morning.

Early peoples in the far northern reaches of Scandinavia made a similar connection between fire and the sun. In the dead of winter there, the sun shines only a few precious hours each day. Scandinavians once lit fires on the shortest day of the year (on or about December 21), in hopes of restoring the sun to its full strength. Some of our Christmas customs, such as lighting candles and burning a Yule log, trace their origins to these early fire/sun rituals.

Season Ticket

Because the earth is tilted in space at a 23 ½-degree angle, different parts of the globe receive more (or less) sun at certain times during the earth's annual 365 ¼-day journey around the sun. You can demonstrate this journey, and the resulting seasons, with the following demonstration.

YOU'LL NEED

- Small lamp, without its shade
- Tape
- Marker
- Globe on a stand

Note: If you don't have a globe, hold a ball or balloon on which you have outlined the continents.

1. Place the lamp in the middle of a table or rug. Mark four positions around the lamp with tape. Label them December, March, June, and September.

2. Place the globe on the tape marked December. Place it on some books to make its top level with the light bulb, if necessary. Make sure the North Pole is facing away from the lamp. (If you are using a decorated balloon or ball, be sure to tilt it like the globe in the drawing.) Slowly turn the globe to show the passage of one day. Which parts of the globe get the most lamplight (sunlight)? Which parts get the least?

3. Place the globe on the other tape markers, making sure to tilt it in the same direction at each stop. Again, check to see what parts of the globe receive the greatest amount of light, and which receive the least.

Sunny Side Up

The sun figures in many words and phrases in English, from Sunday to the Sun King (a name given to Louis XIV of France, who reigned from 1643 to 1715). You and your family and friends can use these words to play a fun game of Charades. Have each player (or team of players) silently act out the words for team members or the whole group to guess.

Here are some "sun" words and phrases to get you started. What others can you add to the list?

EXTRA! EXTRA!

SUMMER SOLSTICE

Did you notice how when the sun shines more directly on North America during the summer months, it shines less directly on Australia and the southern parts of South America and Africa? That explains why we say those regions of the world experience winter when we are enjoying summer. Similarly, you can see why those countries near the equator, the midpoint of the globe, see very little seasonal changes.

WINTER SOLSTICE

SUNBATHE SUNBURN sun porch SUNSCREEN SUNBEAM sunspot sunflower sunglasses Sunday Best

Raised Rays

YOU'LL NEED

- 1 packet active dry yeast
- 1 cup (250 ml) lukewarm water
- 2 tablespoons (30 g) soft butter
- 1 tablespoon (15 ml) sugar
- ½ teaspoon (2.5 ml) salt
- 3 to 3½ cups (375 to 440 g) all-purpose flour
- Egg
- Coarse salt

Many European baked goods—from hearty breads to buttery cookies—are made in the shape of pretzels. The knotted loop shape is a very old symbol, and one that is believed to have once represented the seasonal journey of the sun. (This was before people understood that the earth moves around the sun, and not the other way around.)

Bake a batch of pretzels in recognition of our nearest star and the role it plays in shaping our seasons. Form the dough in the traditional knotted shape, or create rayed suns or other shapes. Be sure to ask an adult to help you with any steps you are not familiar with, as well as when moving the pretzels in and out of the hot oven.

1. Combine the yeast and water in a mixing bowl, stirring to dissolve the yeast. Add the butter, sugar, salt, and 1 ½ cups (200 g) of the flour. Mix with an electric mixer until well blended.

2. Stir in the remaining flour by hand. Turn out the dough onto a floured surface and knead for

GOING, GOING, GONE!

Every so often, something incredible happens to the sun: It disappears in the middle of the day, turning the sky dark and fooling animals and birds into thinking it is night. This is a solar eclipse, and it occurs when the sun, moon, and Earth line up in such a way that the moon completely covers the sun. (Even though the sun is 400 times larger than the moon, it happens to be 400 times farther from the earth, so the two appear the same size.)

Many ancient peoples believed the sun was being eaten by a monster during an eclipse. The Chinese said the Heavenly Dog was responsible. Yugoslavians

about 5 minutes, or until smooth and elastic. Put the dough in a greased bowl, and cover with a kitchen towel. Place the bowl in a warm spot for about an hour, until the dough has risen and doubled in size.

3. Punch down the dough and knead briefly. Divide into 12 pieces. Roll each piece into a rope about 1 inch (2.5 cm) in diameter. Form the ropes into pretzel shapes, or cut into smaller lengths to make your own designs. (Brush the ends of dough pieces with water to help them stick.) Place the finished shapes onto a greased baking sheet. Cover with a towel, and let rise for 30 minutes.

4. Crack the egg in a small bowl, and mix with a spoonful of water. Brush the pretzels with this mixture and sprinkle on coarse salt. Bake the pretzels in a preheated 450°F (230°C) oven for about 12 minutes, or until they are lightly browned. Makes a dozen 6-inch knotted pretzels.

blamed a werewolf, while Hungarians said it was a giant bird.

Some cultures threw rocks or shot arrows into the sky in hopes of frightening away the monster. Others attempted to scare off the intruder with noise, banging drums and setting off fireworks.

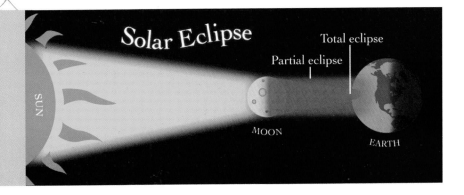

Solar Eclipse

Total eclipse

Partial eclipse

SUN

MOON

EARTH

To Everything There Is a Season

YOU'LL NEED

For the pages:
- Drawing paper, 18 inches by 12 inches (45 cm by 30 cm)

For the covers:
- 2 sheets heavyweight paper, 18 inches by 12 inches (45 cm by 30 cm)
- Ruler
- Pencil
- Paper punch
- Clothespins
- Yarn or thick string
- Large-eyed tapestry needle
- Colored pencils, markers, or paint

Today, most of us rely on calendars to keep track of the days and months of the year. Long ago, people noted the passage of time by watching for changes in the natural world. For example, the appearance of certain plants (like the violets in the story), meant it was safe to start spring planting. Other changes signaled the best time to gather wild nuts in autumn, or when to expect the first snowfall.

You can keep track of seasonal changes with a special nature notebook, one you can refer to year after year. Bind yours in book form, using the traditional Japanese binding shown here.

1. Fold all the sheets of paper into 9-inch by 12-inch (22.5 cm by 30 cm) pages (and covers). Draw a line on one cover sheet 1/2 inch (1.25 cm) from the unfolded edge. Starting 1/2 inch (1.25 cm) from the bottom, measure and mark 12 dots 1 inch (2.5 cm) apart along this line. Punch holes at these marks. Using this page as a guide, punch holes in all the folded sheets.

2. Sandwich the pages between the covers; hold in place with clothespins. Cut a 48-inch (120-cm) length of yarn, and thread the tapestry needle. Leaving a few inches of yarn at the beginning, sew the book with a running stitch from the top of the book to the bottom.

3. Make the last stitch go around the bottom of the book and back through that same last hole in the opposite direction. Now make the yarn go around the spine and through that hole again. Working your way back up the spine, go around the spine at each hole, while also filling in the gaps left by the running stitch.

4. Tie the two loose ends of the yarn together, making sure to go over the top of the book first. Trim the yarn close to the knot. To help the front cover lay flay when open, score (draw a blunt tool along one edge of a ruler) about 1/2 inch (1.25 cm) from the stitching. Decorate the front cover with a favorite design from nature.

NATURE NOTES

What should you record in your nature notebook? You may wish to note the first appearance of robins in spring (or mosquitoes in summer!). Or when it's warm enough to plant tomatoes in the garden, or cold enough to skate on a nearby pond. Each year, as you flip through the book, you'll be reminded of the natural cycles that influence our lives.

The Hare in the Moon

A Tale from India

The moon, be it crescent or full, enlivens the night sky. Not everyone sees the features of a person on the face of the moon, however. Children throughout Asia see the figure of a long-eared rabbit or hare. This tale from India offers one explanation for its presence there.

n a certain time, Hare was friends with Otter, Jackal, and Monkey. On a certain night, the four friends sat admiring the moon, a full moon as round as a rupee and as bright as a thousand flickering flames.

"What a beautiful thing the moon is," Otter sighed.

"Especially when it is full," Jackal agreed.

Hare said, "I have heard that the day after a full moon is a holy day for humans. They eat no food on this day, but offer whatever they have to those who haven't enough food of their own. I was wondering if we shouldn't do the same."

"I'd be willing to give up my dinner if it meant someone less fortunate than I might eat," said Otter.

Jackal nodded in agreement. "Tomorrow let's look for food as usual but not eat anything until sundown."

"And if we meet any beggars, we'll give our food to them instead," Monkey added.

The next day the four friends went their separate ways. Otter spent the day fishing in the slow-moving stream that wound its way through the jungle. He caught three fish, which he dragged, one by one, up onto the bank. "I'll save these for tonight," he said to himself, "unless a hungry beggar stops by, in which case I'll offer them to him."

Monkey went off in search of mangoes. He found a tree laden with ripe fruit and began to pick as many mangoes as his arms could hold. "I'll save these for tonight," he said to himself, "unless a hungry beggar stops by, in which case I'll offer them to him."

Jackal, the scavenger, pawed through trash heaps all day, finally uncovering a big piece of meat. "I don't know why anyone threw this away," he said to himself, "but I'll save it for tonight, unless a hungry beggar stops by, in which case I'll offer it to him."

Like his three friends, Hare set out to find food. As he bent down to pull up tufts of sweet grass, he stopped and sat back on his haunches. "Oh, dear, I hadn't thought of this. Grass is my favorite food, but people do not eat grass. I'll have nothing to offer to beggars," he said.

Then Hare had an idea. "I know. People may not eat grass, but they do eat hares. If a hungry beggar stops by, I'll just offer myself."

Little did Hare realize that Indra, all-knowing god of the sky, was watching him from behind a billowing bank of clouds. Indra was impressed by Hare's generosity. He decided he wanted to meet this compassionate creature in person. Dropping from the sky, Indra disguised himself as a tattered beggar and hobbled up to Hare.

"Greetings to you," said Indra, the beggar man, holding out an empty clay bowl. "Have you any food to spare for a hungry old man?"

Ah, thought Hare, here is my chance. He cleared his throat and said, "If you are hungry, Sir, I would like to offer myself as your meal."

"You would, would you? Hmm, it looks like there is plenty of meat on you. But on a holy day such as this I may not take the life of any animals with my own hands."

"That's not a problem," replied Hare, thinking quickly. "If you'll just make a fire, I'll jump into the flames myself."

The beggar shrugged, then started gathering some dry brush and twigs. He lit the brush, fanning the tiny blaze until it was burning steadily, then added a few logs. In no time the fire was blazing

hot. "I'm ready if you are," the beggar said.

Hare didn't hesitate, but closed his eyes and took a bounding leap, landing in the middle of the roaring flames. "I don't understand!" he exclaimed, his eyes opening wide in wonder. "The flames of the fire are lapping my fur, and I can hear the sizzle and the hiss, yet I feel no heat."

At that moment, the god clapped his hands and the flames vanished into thin air. With a second clap of his hand, his true form was revealed.

"I am Indra," the god said, "and that was not a real fire, just a bit of my magic at work." He smiled. "When I heard you were willing to give your own life in order to better the life of another, I could hardly believe my ears. That is the supreme sacrifice."

Hare blushed, and Indra continued. " Brave Hare, not only were your intentions admirable, but you were as good as your word. Your courage and selflessness shall not go unnoticed."

The god bent down and scooped up a ball of clay from the ground. Patting it into a flat disk, he took a sharp twig and etched the outline of a hare on its surface. Then he threw the disk into the sky. Hare watched as it rose higher and higher into the heavens, until it finally disappeared from sight.

"From this day on," Indra told Hare, "your likeness will be visible when the moon is full. When the people here on earth gaze up and see you, they will be reminded of the sacrifice you were willing to make. They will be inspired to look within their own hearts and share with others less fortunate than they." With that, the god clapped his hands one last time and was gone.

That night, Hare joined his friends Otter, Jackal, and Monkey in the jungle clearing. He told them everything that had happened to him that day.

"Look!" shouted Jackal, as the round moon rose above the tops of the trees. "I can see you, Hare, right there on the face of the moon!"

Otter chimed in. "I can see you, too."

"Don't you look splendid!" added Monkey.

Don't you agree?

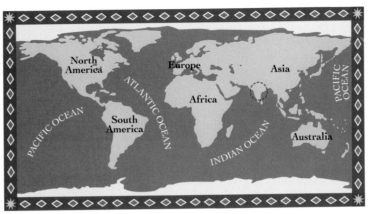

Country: INDIA
Capital: NEW DELHI
Continent: ASIA
Languages: HINDI, ENGLISH

Eye of the Beholder

People in India aren't the only ones who see the silhouette of a hare on the moon. So did the Aztecs of Mexico, and so do the Japanese, the Koreans, and the Chinese, who also see a toad and a boy chopping a tree—though not all at the same time!

While Europeans talk of the man in the moon, some cultures see the features of a woman's face. The Maori (rhymes with flowery) of New Zealand claim this is an old woman who cursed the moon when it went behind a cloud just as she was ready to fetch water. She was banished to the moon, as punishment for her harsh words.

The moon's markings are sometimes described as smudges of dirt.

One tale from Papua, New Guinea, tells of a village where only one woman had the power to make fire. One day while she was away, two curious boys went to her hut, in hopes of discovering her secret. Lifting the lid of a pot, one of the boys released the moon, which began floating away. The boy clambered up a tree to grab the moon before it drifted out of reach, but it was too slippery for him and floated up into the sky. The smudges his dirty hands left are still visible.

What do the markings of the moon look like to you? Invent your own story about the areas of light and dark, or to explain some other aspect of the moon, such as why it changes shape.

Just a Phase

While the earth makes its year-long journey around the sun, the moon is busy revolving around the earth, roughly once a month. We can see much of this journey thanks to reflected light from the sun. (Unlike the sun and the other stars, the moon does not create its own light.)

As the moon travels around the earth, the area lit by the sun slowly changes. We call these changes phases.

Look for the moon in the sky every evening for about a month's time. You won't be able to see the moon when it's new (positioned between the earth and sun, the moon is invisible at this stage), but you can witness its growth from thin crescent to full moon, gradually shrinking back again to invisibility. Are you surprised to find the moon in the sky during the day as well as at night? Where in the sky do you have to look for the different phases?

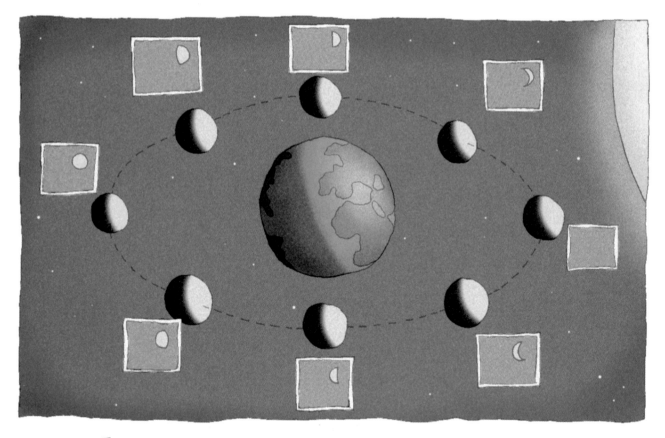

Tricks
of the
Trade

Here's a clever way to remember if the crescent moon you see in the sky is waxing (growing larger) or waning (getting smaller).

When the crescent looks like a "C" shape made with your right hand, it is growing larger (just remember that a greater number of people are right-handed).

When the crescent resembles a "C" shape made by your left hand, it is getting smaller (a smaller number of people are left-handed).

A Year of Moons

The calendar we use today is based on the earth's journey around the sun—a trip that takes about 365 1/4 days. We divide the year into twelve months of 30 and 31 days (the exception being February with 28 or—every four years—29 days).

Long ago, calendars were based on the cycle of the moon's phases. From one new moon to another is about 29 1/2 days, so lunar calendar months alternated between 29 and 30 days (to take care of that half day). There are still some religious calendars in use today, such as the Jewish and Muslim calendars, that are based on this cycle.

There's one problem with the lunar calendar. Because 12 moon cycles equal only 354 days, the lunar calendar does not stay in rhythm with the seasons of the 365-day solar calendar. The Jewish calendar solved this problem by adding a thirteenth month when required. The Muslim calendar makes no adjustments, so it actually moves back 11 days each year. That means a religious festival that takes place on a certain date one year will be 11 days earlier (according to the solar year) the next year, and 11 days earlier than that the following year…and so on.

ANSWER: You would be 8 years old when your birthday fell close to the first day of winter. Thirty-three years would go by before your birthday fell once again in late March.

Hoppy Birthday!

Just think how your birthday would hop backwards from one month to another if you followed the lunar calendar. Say you were born on March 21 (around the first day of spring, according to the solar year). You would celebrate your first birthday on March 10 (that's 21 minus 11, for the eleven days that the lunar calendar moves back each year). Here's a puzzler: By continuing to subtract 11 each year, when would your birthday fall closer to the first day of winter? How old would you be when you celebrated your birthday once again around the 21st of March? See the margin for the answer.

Boxed Beams

The Shan people of Burma describe the moon as a silver hare nestled in a round box. Night after night, the hare pushes the lid open just a little bit, letting more and more of the silvery light show. The hare actually hops out of the box on the night of the full moon — his outline can be seen on the moon's surface. At that point, he returns to the box, closing the lid gradually until it's snug and tight and the box emits no light. Then the process begins again.

Make your own round moon box, decorated with the outline of a silvery hare or some other celestial design. It's just the right size to hold tiny trinkets and treasures.

YOU'LL NEED

- Corrugated cardboard
- Compass, or saucer
- Ruler
- Scissors
- Masking tape
- Newspaper, torn in 1-inch (2.5 cm) strips
- Papier-mâché paste, made from 1 cup (125 g) flour mixed with 1 cup (250 ml) water until smooth
- Sandpaper
- Acrylic paints
- Paintbrush
- Black waterproof marker

1. Using a compass or tracing around a saucer, draw four circles on a piece of cardboard—two the same size for the bottom and top of your box, and two about 1/2 inch (1.25 cm) smaller for the inside of the lid. Measure a strip for the side of the box (the cardboard "ribs" should run width-wise), about three times the diameter of the largest circles. Cut out the four circles and the strip.

2. Form a circular box by taping the strip along the edge of one of the larger circles. Trim the strip so that the two ends meet with no gap or overlap; tape to secure. Make the lid by positioning the two smaller circles in the middle of the remaining large circle; tape in place.

HELPFUL HINT

The best time to make out the features of the moon— man, woman, or hare—is when the full moon is low in the sky. Why is that? Viewing the moon through this thick angle of the earth's atmosphere cuts down on the moon's glare, making it easier to distinguish the light and dark areas.

3. Paste three layers of overlapping newspaper strips on both parts of the box. Cover all edges, taking care to smooth and tuck the strips wherever two pieces of cardboard meet. Place the box in a warm spot for several days until the papier-mâché is completely dry.

4. Sand any rough spots with sandpaper. Paint the box and lid with a light-colored paint; let dry. Pencil designs on the lid and sides of the box, then paint. Let the paint dry, then use the black marker to outline the designs to make them stand out.

A TIME FOR REFLECTION

In the story, Hare describes the custom of sharing food with others the day after a full moon. You can follow the animals' example and volunteer to help some of the people in need in your community.

There are many ways you can get involved. Donate some canned goods to a local food pantry each month, or offer to help out in a soup kitchen. Visit the senior citizens in a nursing home, or give an elderly neighbor a hand with yard work. Read a book to a younger child, or even help someone learn to read.

You may also wish to start some family traditions that coincide with the full moon. Gather together to watch the full moon rise (look to the east just after sunset), or take a short moonlit walk. Bake a batch of full-moon biscuits or cookies (any rolled dough that can be cut out will do). Read aloud some stories and poems about the moon. This is one tradition you can continue when you're all grown up and have a family of your own!

In the Merry Moon of May

While many Native Americans used both the sun and moon to measure the passage of time, each lunar month was given a name for the full moon that appeared at that time. The descriptive names reflected seasonal happenings and local customs. A tribe in the Northeast might refer to March as Moon When Juice Drips from the Trees (referring to the sap of maple trees that flows at this time); desert-dwellers in the Southwest might call it Cactus Blossom Moon.

Some of the colorful names for full moons are still used today. Perhaps you've heard the full moon in September called the Harvest Moon, or the one in October referred to as the Hunter's Moon. Come up with your own full moon names for the months of the year. Which month might you call Birthday Moon?

Glory of the Night

Some of the most fragrant flowers in the garden stay tightly closed during the day. They open only later in the afternoon and evening, perfuming the night air with their sweet scents.

The most magnificent of these late-bloomers is the moonflower. Moonflowers look like white morning glories, only their blossoms are enormous—up to eight inches (20 cm) wide! Each bloom lasts for only one night, but the scent more than makes up for the short performance.

Moonflowers are easy to grow. They do require a long growing season, however, so if summers are short where you live, start seeds indoors 4 to 6 weeks before you can expect the temperatures to stay above 50°F (10°C) at night. Moonflowers don't like their roots disturbed, so take care to remove the root ball in one piece when settling the young plants outdoors in their permanent spot. As moonflowers are vining plants, provide some sort of trellis on which the vine can attach itself.

LAST BUT NOT LEAST

The lemon-scented four-o'clock is another late-bloomer. Its blossoms unfurl—you guessed it!—at four in the afternoon. Flowering tobacco (a relative of the tobacco plant) also waits until late in the day to bloom, as does the evening primrose.

The Moon in Safekeeping

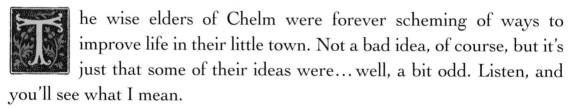

A Jewish Tale from Europe

The full moon lights up more than the night sky; it bathes the earth with its silvery glow.
The townspeople of Chelm (helm), an imaginary place invented by Jewish storytellers of Europe,
wondered if there wasn't some way to harness this light to brighten their streets at night.
Just how they planned on doing this will make you scratch your head in wonder!

The wise elders of Chelm were forever scheming of ways to improve life in their little town. Not a bad idea, of course, but it's just that some of their ideas were… well, a bit odd. Listen, and you'll see what I mean.

One year in October, the wise elders who governed Chelm gathered before their townspeople to discuss the decreasing length of the days. To be sure, the days were gradually growing shorter and shorter. The people of Chelm had begun to complain that it was already dark when they left work each evening, and that they were bumping into one another, even losing their way on the winding cobbled streets.

"Terrible, just terrible," Menachim (men-OCK-him), the wisest of the elders solemnly agreed. "Something must be done about the darkness, and it must be done soon."

But what, what could they do?

"I have a suggestion," said Jacob (YAH-cohb), a merchant whose travels took him to towns and villages far from Chelm. "I have visited places that have oil lamps on every street corner. Street lamps would solve a lot of our problems, I am sure of it."

"Ooh, just think," whispered a member of the audience. "Pinkas the

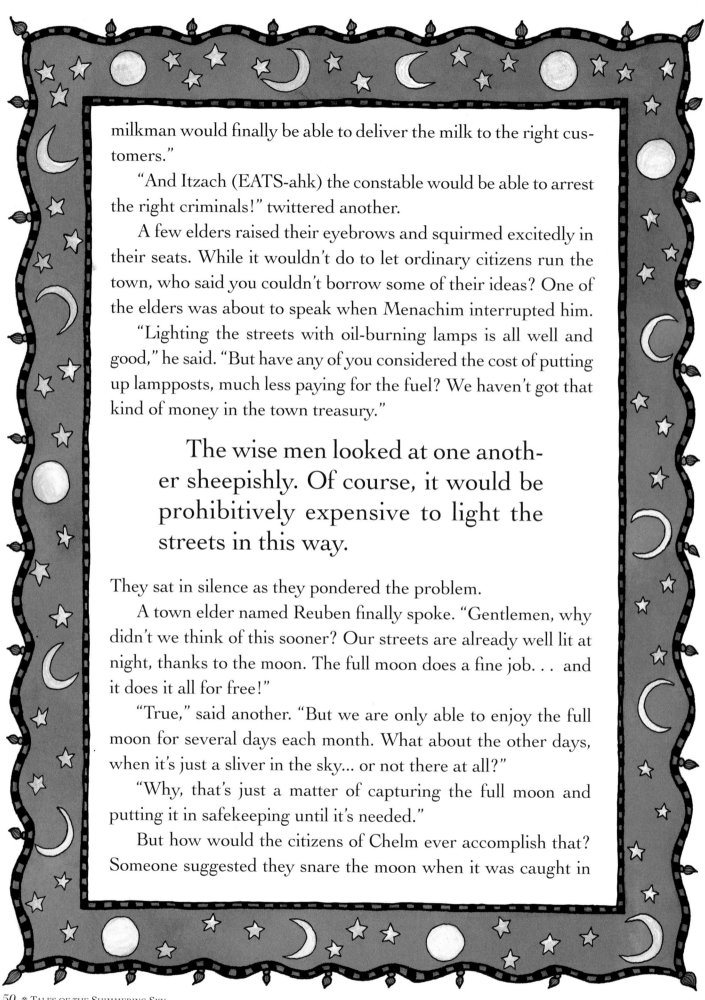

milkman would finally be able to deliver the milk to the right customers."

"And Itzach (EATS-ahk) the constable would be able to arrest the right criminals!" twittered another.

A few elders raised their eyebrows and squirmed excitedly in their seats. While it wouldn't do to let ordinary citizens run the town, who said you couldn't borrow some of their ideas? One of the elders was about to speak when Menachim interrupted him.

"Lighting the streets with oil-burning lamps is all well and good," he said. "But have any of you considered the cost of putting up lampposts, much less paying for the fuel? We haven't got that kind of money in the town treasury."

The wise men looked at one another sheepishly. Of course, it would be prohibitively expensive to light the streets in this way.

They sat in silence as they pondered the problem.

A town elder named Reuben finally spoke. "Gentlemen, why didn't we think of this sooner? Our streets are already well lit at night, thanks to the moon. The full moon does a fine job. . . and it does it all for free!"

"True," said another. "But we are only able to enjoy the full moon for several days each month. What about the other days, when it's just a sliver in the sky... or not there at all?"

"Why, that's just a matter of capturing the full moon and putting it in safekeeping until it's needed."

But how would the citizens of Chelm ever accomplish that? Someone suggested they snare the moon when it was caught in the limbs of a tree. But, no, the net would only get tangled up in the branches and the moon would escape. Someone else noted that the full moon gravitated toward water. Wasn't it true that the moon could be seen shining in lakes and ponds, even puddles, when it was full? Why couldn't they capture it then?

"Brilliant idea," Menachim exclaimed. "We'll fill a barrel with water and wait for the moon to make its way into it. Then we'll bang a lid down on the barrel and have enough light for our streets from now until the end of our days!"

The other elders agreed this was a splendid plan. A brand-new barrel was filled with water and placed in the middle of the town square. When the full moon finally made its appearance one cloudless night, the citizens of Chelm gathered around the barrel to witness the daring capture. The crowd spoke in hushed tones, watching as the big, round moon inched its way up into the sky.

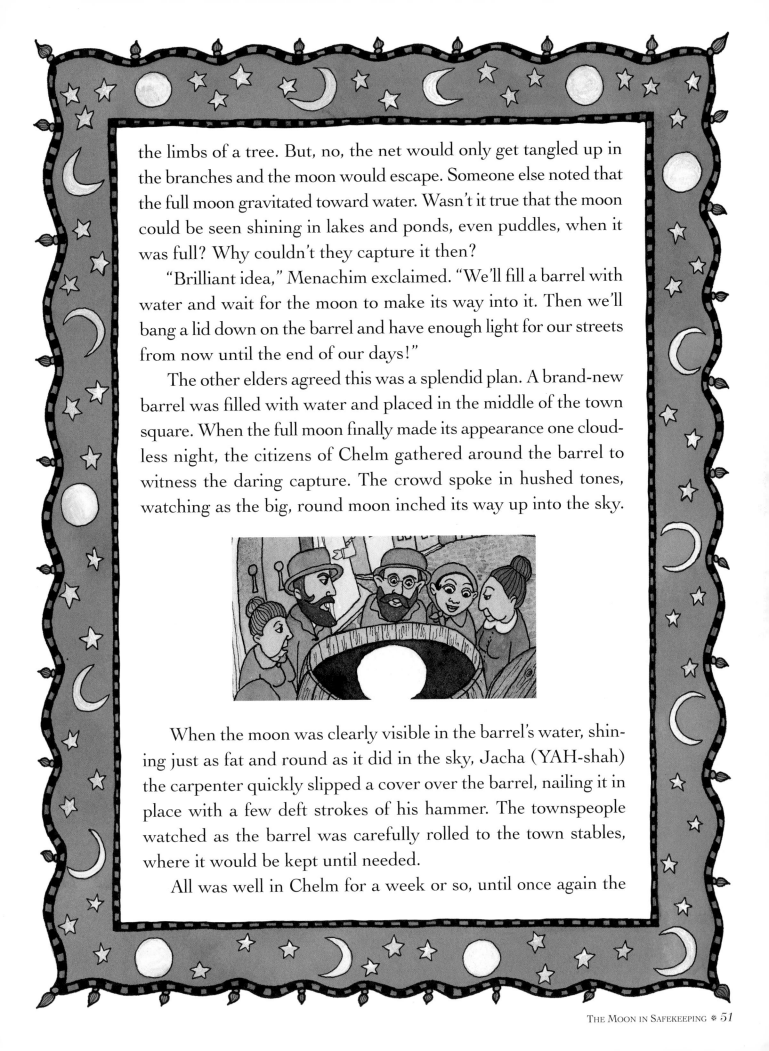

When the moon was clearly visible in the barrel's water, shining just as fat and round as it did in the sky, Jacha (YAH-shah) the carpenter quickly slipped a cover over the barrel, nailing it in place with a few deft strokes of his hammer. The townspeople watched as the barrel was carefully rolled to the town stables, where it would be kept until needed.

All was well in Chelm for a week or so, until once again the dark of night made it difficult to get about. People started bumping into one another and losing their way as they walked home from work. Friends couldn't even be sure whom they were greeting as they passed one another on the street. If the people of Chelm had ever needed to light their town, now was the time.

The town elders ordered the barrel rolled out of the stables, and Jacha the carpenter was called upon to pry off the lid. They spoke not a word, anxiously awaiting the moment when the moon would be loosed to take its place in the sky. But when the lid was removed, the barrel was as black as the night itself. The moon was nowhere to be seen.

"Perhaps it sank to the bottom," offered Reuben. The barrel was tipped over, and the water slowly poured out onto the street.

There was nothing in the barrel. It was completely empty.

"It's not here. It's gone!" exclaimed Menachim. "How could this be? The moon couldn't have just disappeared like that. Someone has stolen it. Someone has stolen our moon!"

The wise elders stood openmouthed in disbelief. Who could have done such a wicked thing? Some greedy miser who wanted the moon all for himself? Thieves from another town who had stolen their idea for lighting the streets?

"What fools we were," lamented the elders of Chelm. "We should have guarded our moon more carefully." Next time they would, they agreed. Next time they would.

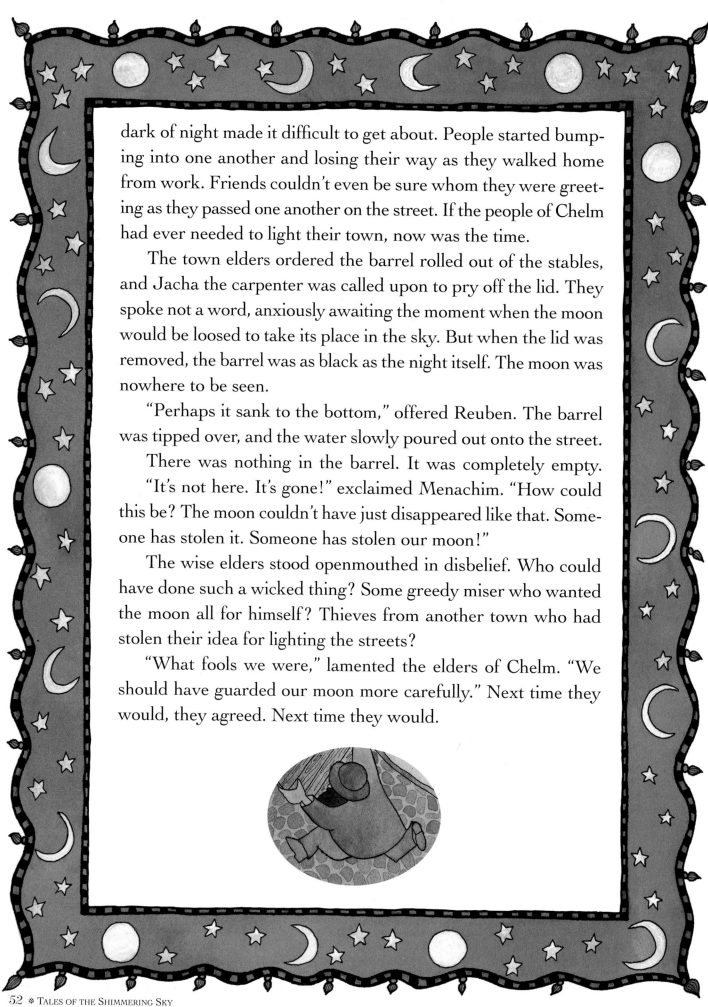

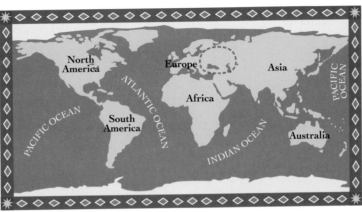

Region: EASTERN EUROPE
Continent: EUROPE
Languages: YIDDISH, HEBREW

Ripple Effect

If you've ever seen the moon's reflection in water, you may have been taken in by the same visual trickery that fooled the townspeople of Chelm. The perfectly round circle of light can look remarkably like it is floating in the water. Fables about such reflections are found all over the world. Just as in this tale, in many stories the characters foolishly believe they can capture the moon while it's in the water.

In one Turkish tale, a man goes to draw water from his well one evening and is startled to see the reflection of the moon in the water. Thinking the moon has fallen in, the man tries to fish it out. He puts a huge hook on the end of a fishing line and lowers it into the well. When the hook gets caught between two rocks, the man is sure he has snared the moon. He tugs and tugs with all his might, but the fishing line breaks, flinging him flat on his back. Seeing the moon up in the sky, the foolish fellow congratulates himself for returning it to its rightful place.

Tidal Waves

There actually is a strong connection between the moon and water. The moon is the strongest of the three gravitational forces that create ocean tides. (The other two are the earth's own rotation and the gravitational pull from the sun.) This pull creates two high tides on earth each day, one every 12 hours and 25 minutes. Midway between each of the high tides is a low tide.

If you live near the ocean, you may have noticed that the high and low tides at certain times of the month are higher and lower than usual. These are known as spring tides (yet has nothing to do with the season spring), and they occur just after the moon is full and after its new phase. When the high and low tides hardly differ, this is called a neap tide. This happens just after the moon goes through its first and last quarter phases.

TAKE A BITE OUT OF THE MOON

The moon has inspired its share of edible delicacies. In China, round buns filled with spicy bean paste, called mooncakes, are eaten in celebration of the moon's birthday, on the eighth day of the eighth month of the Chinese calendar. The French start their day with croissants (kwah-SAHWN), buttery pastries that are shaped like a crescent moon. Swedish children snack on delicate sandwich cookies they call cherry half moons, which resemble the moon during its quarter phase.

Blue Cheese, Maybe

Perhaps you've heard the expression "the moon is made of green cheese." Did people ever really believe this was what the moon was made from? Not likely. They were probably thinking how the moon looks like a wheel of pale, unripened cheese. Green cheese is just another name for unripened cheese.

Speaking of cheese, a delicious stand-in for the moon can be made from it. Choose one of the blue cheeses, such as French Roquefort (ROAK-for) or English Stilton, to make a cheese ball that bears more than a passing resemblance to the earth's celestial companion!

YOU'LL NEED

- 3/4 cup (100 g) blue cheese, crumbled
- 4-ounce (113 g) package of cream cheese, at room temperature
- 1 tablespoon (15 ml) fresh parsley, minced
- 1 teaspoon (5 ml) Worcestershire sauce
- 1/4 cup (30 g) chopped walnuts

Combine all the ingredients in a mixing bowl, using your hands to form a ball. Serve with plain crackers, or spread on celery sticks for a crunchy treat. Makes a 4-inch (10 cm) ball.

Once in a Blue Moon

Then there's the blue moon, as in "once in a blue moon." Something that happens "once in a blue moon" is something that doesn't happen very often. This quaint expression actually refers to two different natural phenomena.

A true blue moon occurs when the dust particles in the earth's atmosphere are just right (usually following a volcanic eruption or wide-spread forest fire). When the moon is viewed low on the horizon through this haze, it has a bluish cast.

Two full moons in the same calendar month are also called blue moons. Blue moons such as these occur roughly every two and one-half years, most often during those months that have 31 days.

Loony Loops

Don't judge the foolish elders of Chelm too harshly. You may find yourself fooled by the following classic trick. It sounds simple enough: What do you get when you cut a looped strip in half? If you think the answer is two thinner looped strips, you're right... and you're wrong!

Once you've learned the secret behind these special loops, stage a demonstration for your family and friends. Can any of them figure out how the cut strips will end up?

YOU'LL NEED

- Plastic garbage bag, cut into 3 strips, each about 4 inches (10 cm) wide
- Scissors
- Tape

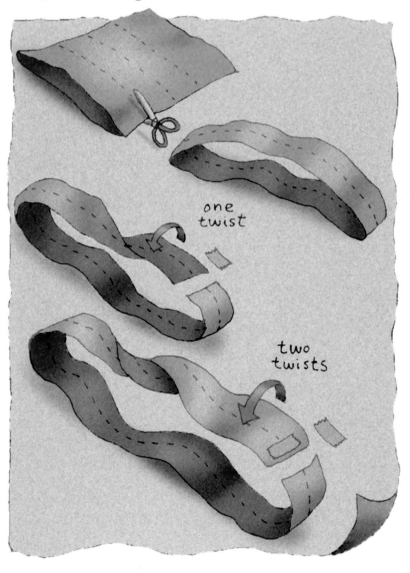

one twist

two twists

1. Pick up one of the strips. Separate the two layers to show it is one continuous loop. What do you think will happen if you cut the strip in half lengthwise? Not surprisingly, you end up with two separate loops.

2. Take another strip, only this time cut the loop at one side seam. Mark the outside of one end of the strip with a piece of tape. Twist this end of the strip so that the tape mark no longer shows. (You have made a half, or 180 degree, twist in the strip.) Tape the two ends of the strip together. Now cut the strip in half lengthwise. Surprised?

3. Cut the third strip and mark the outside of one end of it as you did in Step 2. This time give the strip two twists before taping the ends together (the marking tape should show on top). Cut the strip in half lengthwise to reveal yet another amazing end result.

Let There Be Light!

Imagine what the townspeople of Chelm would have thought of electricity—and the ease with which we light up our lives at the flick of a switch.

While we can't capture the moon and harness its light, you can have the next best thing with this fun lampshade decorated with crescent moons and stars.

YOU'LL NEED

- Light-colored lampshade, made from paper or smooth fabric
- Stiff paper, such as oak tag or index cards
- Scissors
- Masking tape
- Small sponge, about 1 inch (2.5 cm) square
- Acrylic paint
- Paper plate

1. Cut 8 to 12 crescent moon and star shapes from stiff paper. Tape the shapes to the lampshade, using small, rolled pieces of masking tape applied to the back of the cut-outs.

2. Squirt some acrylic paint onto the paper plate. Add a small amount of water to the paint to make it the consistency of thick cream. Dip the sponge in the paint, blotting off the excess on a piece of scrap paper. Dab paint around the shapes on the lampshade, using quick, light movements. Paint coverage should be even, but not thick.

3. When the paint is completely dry, remove the shapes carefully. Put the shade back on the lamp. Let there be light!

Universal Symbols

Since the beginning of time, man has been drawing representations of the heavenly bodies on every available surface, from cave walls to finely woven tapestries. The simplest, and most usual, symbol for the moon is a crescent. (This helps distinguish it from the sun, which is usually shown as a plain round circle.) The crescent is often shown on its side, making it look like a cradle or a big smile!

Turn the symbols for the moon, sun, and stars into a colorful banner to hang in your room. You don't even need to know how to sew, as this wall hanging is made entirely from glued felt pieces.

YOU'LL NEED

- Felt (by the yard and smaller pieces), in assorted colors
- Scissors
- Fabric glue
- Dowel
- String

1. Plan your banner on paper first, if you like, or design it as you go.

2. Cut a large shape from felt for the background. Fold the top edge over to make a pocket for the dowel; glue to secure.

In the Dark

Just as the moon, earth, and sun occasionally are perfectly aligned, creating a solar eclipse (for more on this, see pages 32–33), the earth sometimes comes between the sun and full moon, resulting in a lunar eclipse. When this happens, the bright full moon gradually becomes darker and darker, but even when the eclipse is total, the moon is faintly visible. That's because the moon, normally reflecting light directly from the sun, reflects a small amount of light that's bouncing off the earth. This redirected light contains more red, often turning the eclipsed moon a dramatic coppery color. Quite the sight!

3. Glue various moon, sun, and star shapes to the banner background. Let the glue dry.

Slip the dowel in the banner's pocket, tie a piece of string to each end of the dowel, and hang.

The crescent moon is featured on the flags of many countries of the world. This sliver of a moon represents Islam, the religion practiced by Muslims all over the world. Look for the crescent (often accompanied by a star or stars) on dozens of different flags, including those of Turkey, Pakistan, Algeria, and Singapore.

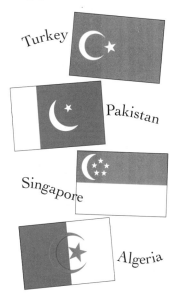

Turkey

Pakistan

Singapore

Algeria

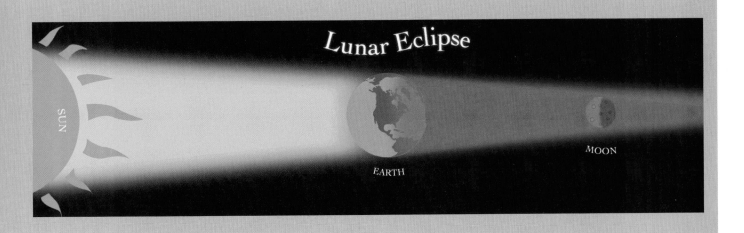

Lunar Eclipse

SUN

EARTH

MOON

Great Bear

The Big Dipper, one of the best known star patterns in the sky, is visible year-round in much of North America. Over the course of the year, its seven stars gradually change their orientation, making a complete circle around the celestial North Pole. This tale, told by the Micmac Indians of eastern Canada, offers one explanation for this movement.

The summer sky was growing darker by the minute, and only the brightest stars were visible. Old Woman sat on the ground facing a small group of children. She looked at each child, one after another, then closed her eyes. This was the signal for the children to sit still. When all was quiet, Old Woman opened her eyes and began to speak.

"This is the story of Great Bear, who roams the northern sky, right up there where you are looking. See those four stars?" Old Woman asked, turning her body and pointing to the stars that form the bowl of the constellation known as the Big Dipper. "Those are Great Bear's four paws. And this is the story of what happened to her when she climbed out of her cave one spring."

"Where is her cave?" asked Little Boy. Little Boy is always interrupting with questions. Old Woman says she doesn't mind. She says that without questions there would be no answers.

Old Woman smiled. "Journey up with your eyes. Do you find a little, curving group of stars, with a wide opening? That is Great Bear's cave."

The children searched the sky for the constellation many call Corona Borealis (cor-OH-nah bore-ee-AL-uss), or the Northern Crown. The older children murmured excitedly when they found it.

"Tonight, you are seeing Great Bear as she appears in summer," Old Woman said. "In late spring, when she crawls out of her cave she is much

higher in the sky. And right behind her trail seven hunters."

"I see only three," said Little Boy.

"Those are the first three," Old Woman began. "There are four more hunters lagging a bit further behind."

"Who are the hunters?" asked Bigger Boy. "Are they men, or boys?" he added hopefully.

"They are neither," Old Woman said. "They are birds. First in line is Robin, followed by Chickadee, and then Moose Bird, who is not really much of a hunter. Then come Pigeon, Blue Jay, Owl, and Saw-whet."

Bigger Boy was curious to know why so many birds were hunting together. Old Woman said, "Chickadee knows that birds don't have much of a chance on their own against Great Bear. Working together is much more likely to bring them success."

"It is like that with us, too," said Little Boy.

"It is," agreed Old Woman.

She continued with her story. "All summer long, the seven hunters fly after Great Bear. They never let her out of their sight. She changes course, swinging down from her high point in the sky, hoping to trick the birds. But she can't shake them from her trail. They keep right behind her. But some of the birds are beginning to tire of the hunt. The two owls are the first to decide they have had enough, and fly off. The next to disappear are Blue Jay and Pigeon."

"Where do they go?" asked the girl they called Only Girl.

"Oh, this way and that," replied Old Woman. "We can't see them because they dip below the mountains."

"If there are only three birds left, the littlest of the three, does that mean Great Bear is safe?" asked Little Boy.

"Nooo, Littlest Boy," Old Woman said, tenderly. "Because Great Bear is growing tired herself. She is not sure how much longer she can keep going.

> And so it happens:
> In mid autumn, Great Bear is too
> tired to run any further.

Rising up on her hind legs, she makes one last attempt to scare the birds away with her menacing growl and swiping claws. But she doesn't realize that she is making herself an even easier target. Robin takes aim with his bow and fires an arrow which strikes Great Bear right in her heart. She falls on her back, dead."

The children sat perfectly still. Even Little Boy was too stunned to speak. While hunting was very much a part of their lives, the children had been all secretly hoping Great Bear would outwit the birds.

Old Woman let a moment pass in silence, then she resumed her tale. "It is Robin who climbs up on Great Bear to make sure she is dead. He gets some blood on his breast, which never washes out. There is a lot of blood. It drips from Great Bear's wound, landing on some maple trees below."

"That's why the maples turn red in autumn!" Little Boy exclaimed.

"That is why," echoed Old Woman.

"So did the birds finally get their meal?" Only Girl wanted to know.

"They did. Moose Bird had fallen behind right before the kill, but he showed up just as the others were roasting Great Bear on the fire. Moose Bird is like that. He shows up after everyone else has done all the work. That is where he gets his name—He-who-comes-in-at-the-last-moment."

"Is that the end of the story?" asked Little Boy.

"Not quite" replied Old Woman. "During the winter months, Great Bear's skeleton floats back up into the sky. Outwardly, Great Bear appears to be dead, but her spirit lives on. Her spirit returns to the cave, where it spends the winter, to be reborn the following spring."

"Just like the bears in our woods do," Bigger Boy said.

"That's right," Old Woman nodded. "Each autumn the bears of our woods return to their caves, where they spend the winter in a deep, deathlike sleep. They awaken and come to life in spring, and the cycle starts all over again."

"Is the story over now?" Little Boy wanted to know.

Old Woman looked at the children seated before her. A faint smile was barely visible on her wrinkled face. "The story never ends," she said at last.

Nation: MICMAC
Region: EASTERN CANADA
Continent: NORTH AMERICA
Language: ALGONQUIAN

Seven Up

The seven stars of the Big Dipper are actually part of a much larger constellation, or star picture, known as Ursa Major (that's "Big Bear" in Latin). Just by chance, many different peoples around the world associated these stars with a bear, even though they were "seeing" somewhat different bears. Can you spot the Big Dipper in the full constellation?

The Big Dipper is one of the few star patterns that actually looks like its name. It really does resemble a giant dipper (another name for a ladle). Why do we call it the Big Dipper? Because there is a similar but smaller pattern of stars in the sky. We call this one—you guessed it!—the Little Dipper. (For more on where to find the Little Dipper, see page 66.)

The British have a completely different name for the Big Dipper. They call it the Plough (plow). In parts of France—a country famous for its fine food—people call it the Saucepan. Other European countries think of the Big Dipper as a cart or wagon, while ancient Chinese art shows the stars as a chariot in which the Emperor of Heaven rides.

Seeing Stars

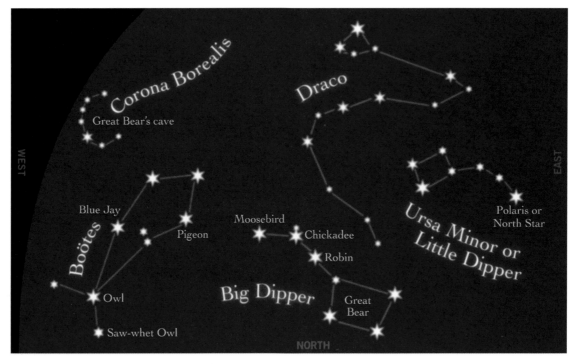

If you'd like to find the stars mentioned in "Great Bear," all you have to do is go outdoors on a clear, moonless night during the summer months.

Stand facing north. (Need some help finding north? Use a compass, or try this simple trick: Look toward the part of the sky where the sun rises in the morning. Now make a quarter of a turn to your left. That's north.) The Big Dipper is easy to spot. At this time of year, its long handle curves to the left.

Once you've spotted the Big Dipper, draw an imaginary line from the top outermost star in its bowl. That will take you to the star on the handle end of the Little Dipper. This is Polaris (poh-LAHR-iss), also known as the North Star. The Little Dipper (also called Ursa Minor, or "Little Bear") doesn't figure in the story, but the constellation can help you find the other stars.

With your eyes, "draw" a line from Polaris to the opposite end of the Little Dipper…and beyond. You will come to Corona Borealis, or the Northern Crown, which is Great Bear's cave in the story. Boötes (boh-OH-teez), a big constellation shaped like a kite, is next to the Crown. The two owls, pigeon, and blue jay of the story are represented by four of Boötes's nine stars.

Following Directions

Polaris is a handy star to know when you're trying to orient yourself outdoors. When you are facing Polaris, you are facing north. Because most star charts use north (and south, its opposite) as reference points, it's helpful to know those directions.

Of course, you can always find north with a compass, such as this homemade one.

1. Draw a circle slightly larger than the sewing needle on the styrofoam tray; cut it out with scissors, and set aside.

YOU'LL NEED

- Large, shallow container of water
- Styrofoam tray (not from raw meat)
- Scissors
- Strong magnet
- Sewing needle
- Tape

2. Rub the needle along the magnet—always in the same direction, from the pointed end to the eye end—at least 30 times. Tape it to the center of the styrofoam circle.

3. Carefully place the circle on the water's surface. Watch it turn until it comes to rest. The pointed end of the needle will be pointing north.

STAR OF THE NORTH

Polaris (Latin for "of the pole") is located near the celestial North Pole. Many of its other names refer to its location in the sky. We call it the North Star, as did the Maya of Mexico. The Navajo call it North Fire; the Lapps refer to it as Nail of the North.

Because it points north, Polaris once played an important role in navigation. That's where it gets another of its names, Lodestar (from Middle English for "Star That Shows the Way").

Tricks *of the* Trade

A good time to stargaze is just as it's getting dark. Why is that? Because only the very brightest stars are visible at first, making it much easier to spot many of the constellations. You'll want to stay out until it's really dark, however, so that you can see the Milky Way (for more on this, see page 79) and marvel at the thousands of visible stars. To make the most of your stargazing, keep in mind the following:

☀ Make yourself comfortable on a reclining chair, or on a waterproof ground sheet. It's a lot easier on your neck.

☀ Take a star chart with you, and a flashlight covered with a piece of red cellophane or plastic wrap. This gives you enough light to read a chart by, but keeps your eyes adapted to the dark.

☀ Record some of your observations in a notebook. (See page 34 for a nature notebook you can make yourself.) List the constellations you've identified, as well as other things you've witnessed, such as shooting stars and planets.

☀ Try to find a spot away from distracting lights, such as street lamps and house lights.

☀ Dress warmly, and take some blankets with you. Even in the middle of summer, you can get chilled lying still for long periods.

All the Better to See You With

Stargazing takes on a new dimension when you view the sky through a pair of binoculars. For best results, rest your elbows on the arms of a chair, or lean against a wall, to steady the binoculars.

Even more of the night sky's wonders come to life with a telescope. With the extra magnification, you can clearly see the craters of the moon, and such marvels as the rings around Saturn.

Some telescopes are amazingly powerful, and have done much to further our understanding of the universe. Thanks to the Hubble Space Telescope, launched into orbit around the earth in 1990, some 19 million stars have been identified and catalogued!

Starry, Starry Night

On a clear, dark night you can see as many as two to three thousand stars in the sky—that is, without binoculars or a telescope. That's only counting about half of them. You can't see the stars that are hidden by the earth beneath your feet. People living below the equator in the Southern Hemisphere see those stars.

Once you've found the stars mentioned in "Great Bear" you may wish to discover some other star groupings. There are plenty to choose from: There are 88 officially recognized constellations, from Andromeda to Vulpecula. Different constellations become visible as the earth orbits the sun over the course of the year. (For a tale and activities about some of the stars visible during the winter months, see pages 74 through 80.)

DID YOU KNOW?

Most of the constellations have Greek or Roman names, while many individual stars go by Arabic names.

THE SUMMER SKY

NORTH

PERSEUS

CASSIOPEIA

ANDROMEDA

CEPHEUS

Delta Cephei

URSA MINOR

Polaris

URSA MAJOR

Mizar

CANES VENATICI

LEO

Deneb

CYGNUS

Vega

LYRA

DRACO

DELPHINUS

HERCULES

BOOTES

Arcturus

CORONA BOREALIS

PEGASUS

EAST

AQUARIUS

Altair

AQUILA

SERPENS (CAUDA)

OPHIUCHUS

SERPENS (CAPUT)

VIRGO

Spica

WEST

LIBRA

CAPRICORNUS

SAGITTARIUS

Antares

SCORPIUS

SOUTH

Showing the Way

Did you know that the Big Dipper once served as a directional guide to American slaves in the 19th century?

From the 1830s to 1865, the year slavery was abolished, untold numbers of black slaves made their way to the free northern states and Canada along the Underground Railroad. This was not an actual railroad, but the descriptive name for the network of people working together to help the runaway slaves. Some people offered the slaves food, or hiding places in their homes; others ferried them across rivers in the middle of the night.

Without road signs or maps—or even compasses—to guide them, the runaways relied on the stars to guide them in the right direction. With the Drinking Gourd—their name for the Big Dipper—in front of them, the slaves knew they were heading north to freedom.

A simple song called "Follow the Drinkin' Gourd" was sung at the time. It offered other helpful clues for a successful journey. Here's how it goes:

Chorus

Fol-low _____ the drink-in' gourd,

old man is a-wait-in' for to car-ry you to

Verse

1. When the sun comes up, and the first quail calls

1. old man is a-wait-in' for to car-ry you to

{repeat chorus}

2. The river bank makes a mighty good road;
   The dead trees will show you the way.
   Left foot, peg foot, travelin' on,
   Follow the drinkin' gourd.

{repeat chorus}

3. The river ends between two hills,
   Follow the drinkin' gourd.
   There's another river on the other side,
   Follow the drinkin' gourd.

Fol-low _____ the drink-in' gourd _ For the

free-dom, If you fol-low the drink — in' gourd.

Fol-low _____ the drink-in' gourd _ For the

free-dom, If you fol-low the drink — in' gourd.

{repeat chorus}

4. When the great big river meets the little river,
   Follow the drinkin' gourd.
   For the old man is awaitin' for to carry you to freedom
   If you follow the drinkin' gourd.

Follow the drinkin' gourd, follow the drinkin' gourd...

There are all sorts of hints cleverly disguised in the song's words. Take the very first verse: "When the sun comes back and the first quail calls," are code words for springtime. That was the best time for the slaves to travel north. Later in that verse it mentions "the old man" who is waiting. Legend has it that this was Peg Leg Joe, a one-legged sailor who was a free black man. He met the slaves at the end of their journey, ferrying them across the Ohio River to the free states on the other side. (Did you catch the other mention of him in the second verse—"left foot, peg foot"?)

The river that "ends between two hills," in the third verse, is the Tombigbee River in Mississippi. "There's another river on the other side" refers to the Tennessee River.

The "great big river" of the last verse is the mighty Ohio River itself.

Wild Blue Yonder

The ancient peoples of Mexico were avid astronomers. The Maya, whose civilization spanned from 1500 BC to 900 AD, used their observations to create an amazingly accurate calendar. The Aztec, who lived in central Mexico from around 1100 to 1520, also watched the sky closely.

The Aztec had an interest in riddles. Not surprisingly, astronomy figured into a number of them. You might be able to figure out what is meant by the following puzzler:

I am a blue bowl filled with popcorn. What am I?

Give up? The answer is the night sky filled with stars!

Make up a fresh batch of popcorn to enjoy while you're stargazing. Sprinkle it with a spicy topping in honor of the ancient astronomers of Mexico.

YOU'LL NEED

- Popcorn
- Melted butter
- 1/4 teaspoon (1.25 ml) chile powder
- 1/4 teaspoon (1.25 ml) garlic powder
- 1/4 teaspoon (1.25 ml) salt

Pop the corn kernels according to package directions. Toss with melted butter. Combine the remaining ingredients in an empty salt shaker. Shake the spices liberally over the hot popcorn. Serve in a blue bowl!

YOU'LL NEED

- 6 3-inch (7.5-cm) squares of medium-weight paper
- Glue
- Needle and decorative thread

Points of View

Stars shine with a steady light, but because we view them through the earth's atmosphere, they appear to twinkle and shimmer. That's why artists throughout history have drawn stars with radiating points. Some stars are shown with as few as four points; others have too many points to count. (For another paper star project—one with nearly 100 points!—see page 80.)

This unusual six-pointed star is made from individual squares of paper, each folded separately and joined with glue. Experiment with fewer or more squares to make stars with different point configurations.

1. Fold one paper square in half diagonally. Crease well, then unfold. Fold the square in half horizontally, then in half vertically; opening after each fold. Bring all four corners up and in toward the center, letting the unit fold in on itself along the crease lines.

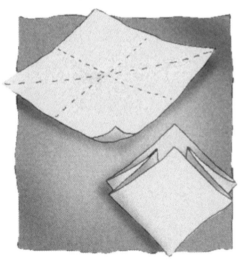

2. Fold the remaining squares according to the instructions in Step 1. Glue the flat faces of two units together, pressing them together firmly until they bond. Continue adding units, gluing the last unit both to the one before it and to the one that follows, forming a star shape.

3. Poke a tiny hole in one of the glued faces with the needle. Tie a length of decorative thread through the hole, then hang.

The Boastful Star

A Tale from Polynesia

Among the delights of the winter sky is a cluster of stars known as the Pleiades (PLEE-ah-deez). Although European tradition says there are seven stars in this tiny group, some cultures insist there are only six. Just how these stars came to be is the subject of this tale from the Hervey Islands, which lie about 1500 miles (2400 km) east of Fiji.

Long, long ago, there was one star in the sky brighter than all the others. It wasn't enough for this star to know he was the brightest. He spent most of his time boasting about his clear, white light, and how no other star in the sky even came close to his brilliance.

"I'm dazzling, that's all there is to it," the star said every chance he got. "Not only that, I am the most beloved of all the stars. Why, if the rest of the stars suddenly disappeared, no one would even miss them!"

The other stars in the sky did their best to ignore this boastful talk. So did Tane-mahuta (tah-nay mah-HOO-tah), the god who reigned over celestial lights. But when the conceited star claimed that he was worthy of the kind of admiration given to the gods, Tane was more than a little annoyed. And when the star said outright, " What has Tane got that I haven't? I'm easily twice as important than he is!" Tane lost all patience with the arrogant star.

"I've had it with this braggart's ridiculous claims," he said to a group of stars gathered before him. "I don't think I can stand another day of his nonsense."

"What do you propose to do?" asked one of the younger stars.

"Banish him from our part of the sky," Tane said. "Only he won't go willingly, so I'm going to need some help. Aldebaran (al-DEB-eh-rahn)," he said

to the large star that shines in the constellation known as Taurus, "you've suffered your share of humiliation. Will you help me?"

Aldebaran had long been overshadowed by the boastful star, as their homes in the sky were close to one another. Aldebaran's soft orange glow was nearly drowned out by his neighbor's glare. "Count me in," he said.

Sirius (SEER-ee-us), the second brightest star in the sky at that time, came forward. He is the blazing star in the constellation called Canis Major. "I'll help, too. I was the brightest star in the sky before this show-off came along. Not only that, many of my fellow stars are being completely ignored, thanks to this snooty star. I'm not going to sit back any longer and let him get all the glory for the night sky!"

The three allies set off at once. The boastful star saw them coming and guessed what they had in mind.

He ran off in the direction of the heavenly stream, where he dove into the water and disappeared from view.

"We'll never be able to spot him underwater," Tane cried. "Oh, it's no use. We'll never get rid of him now."

"I'll divert the stream," Sirius said, and he made the river, the band of stars known as the Milky Way, veer from its normal course. There in the original stream bed crouched the cowering star, who leapt up and ran off as fast as he could go.

Tane and his star helpers gave chase once again. It looked

as if they would never catch up with the boastful star when he stopped and turned to face his pursuers. He wasn't going to give up without proving once and for all that he was the most magnificent star in the entire sky. Swelling with pride, the star began to grow — larger and larger — until he could grow no larger and burst with a blinding explosion and deafening bang.

When the stardust had settled, Tane and his helpers saw that in place of the once brilliant star were six smaller stars. The six fragments admitted defeat, and limped back to their home in the sky under the watchful eyes of Tane. The god felt certain he would never have any trouble from them again.

The other stars in the sky all rejoiced. No longer would Aldebaran's close neighbor outshine him. And Sirius could once claim title as the brightest star in the sky. He'd be sure never to brag about it, though.

As for Mata-riki (mah-tah REE-kee), or "Little Eyes," as the six stars are called, they were still convinced they were the most beautiful stars in the sky, only now they were smart enough to keep their opinion to themselves.

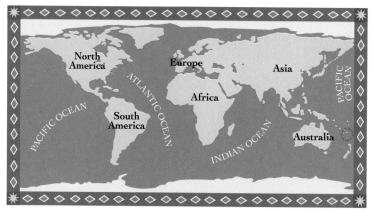

Country: HERVEY ISLANDS
Region: SOUTH PACIFIC
Language: POLYNESIAN

At Sixes and Sevens

Many cultures around the world have shown great interest in the tiny cluster of stars we call the Pleiades. As mentioned in the introduction to "The Boastful Star," not all cultures say there are six stars in the cluster. The name Pleiades comes from the ancient Greeks, who referred to the cluster as the Seven Sisters. The Dutch tell a story describing them as a baker and his six daughters; to the Romanians, they are a hen and her brood of six chicks.

Because only six stars (some people claim to see as many as nine) can usually be seen with the naked eye, many cultures have invented stories to explain the absence of the seventh star. How did the idea of seven stars come about? Some people think it's because the Pleiades look like a miniature Big Dipper,

which has seven stars. (For more on the Big Dipper, see the tale and activities beginning on page 60.)

Cast of Characters

The stars of "The Boastful Star" are visible in the Northern Hemisphere during the winter months. Depending on where you live, you should be able to find them from December until April.

Facing south, look first for one of the most distinctive constellations of the winter sky—Orion (oh-RYE-un). Orion's three-star belt gives him away. Orion doesn't figure in the story, but he'll help you find the other members of the cast.

Notice how the three stars of Orion's belt angle up from left to right. Following that angle, trace an imaginary line to the right until you spot a fuzzy cluster of stars. This is the Pleiades (on the bull's shoulder in the constellation Taurus.) How many stars do you see? (Check to see how many are visible through a pair of binoculars!)

Midway between Orion's belt and the Pleiades is a bright reddish star. This is Aldebaran, which marks the bull's eye in the constellation Taurus.

Nearly the same distance from Orion's belt in the other direction (drawing a line down from the belt) is Sirius, the sky's brightest star. Bluish-white, Sirius is located in the constellation known as Canis Major, or Big Dog.

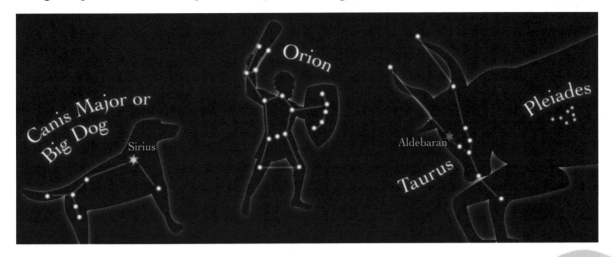

THE GREAT WHITE WAY

The celestial stream in the story is the band of stars we call the Milky Way. Not surprisingly, many cultures described the Milky Way as a river. What we see of this enormous spiral in space—a structure called a galaxy, and the one in which our solar system is located—does resemble a meandering stream.

The ancient Persians described it as a trail of straw, accidentally dropped by a straw thief. The Pawnee Indians of the central United States see it as a cloud of dust kicked up by the buffalo galloping across the sky. The Pokomo people of East Africa think it looks more like a ribbon of smoke from a campfire. Other

cultures think of the Milky Way as the road traveled by the dead, on their way to an afterlife in the heavens.

The Milky Way is beautiful to behold. Visible year-round, look for it on a truly dark night, for the milky band of stars, gas, and dust is faint and easily obscured by light.

Thousand Points of Light

The boastful star of the story was convinced he was the most brilliant star in the sky. It seems he hadn't met this Polish paper star! Usually hung at Christmas, this impressive decoration is also known as a porcupine ball (thanks to its many quill-like points).

Polish paper stars are often made from white tissue paper, but you can experiment with other materials, such as thin colored paper or thick aluminum foil. You may need fewer or more pattern pieces depending on the thickness of the paper and the size of the circles you cut.

YOU'LL NEED

- White tissue paper, cut into 12 5-inch (12.5 cm) circles
- Scissors
- Thin cardboard, such as an index card
- Tape
- White glue
- Needle and thread

1. Divide and mark one of the paper circles in eighths. Place this circle on top of several other circles. Cut along the lines, through all the layers, stopping about one-third of the way from the center. (Repeat as often as necessary to cut all the circles.)

2. Roll a 3-inch (7.5 cm) square of thin cardboard into a cone shape; tape to hold. Wrap one segment of a tissue paper circle around this cone. Secure with a tiny amount of glue. Wrap and glue the remaining segments. Complete the remaining circles the same way.

3. Thread the needle, knotting the end with a large knot. Pass the needle first through a small scrap of cardboard, then through the very center of all the tissue circles, one after another. Finish with another cardboard scrap. Pull gently on the thread, bunching the pointed circles into a ball. Knot the end of the thread securely, then tie the remaining portion into a hanging loop.

Sun
Mercury
Venus
Earth
Mars
Jupiter
Saturn
Uranus
Neptune
Pluto

Sky Wanderers

Not all of the lights in the night sky are stars. Some are airplanes (these are usually fast-moving colored lights, accompanied by faint noise), others are man-made satellites. Still others are planets.

That's right — some of the planets of our solar system are visible with the naked eye. In fact, ancient astronomers long ago identified Mercury, Venus, Mars, Jupiter, and Saturn. They noticed that these celestial lights were different than stars. While stars predictably appeared in certain parts of the sky (depending on the time of night and season), the planets wandered about. A planet might be visible in the morning sky for a while, then appear in the evening sky, or wander off altogether. In fact, that's where the word planet comes from — from the Greek word for "wanderer."

Astronomers have since discovered more planets revolving around our sun, bringing the total, to date, to nine. Like our earth, many of the planets have moons (Saturn has at least 18!). Unlike our earth, there are no signs of life on any of the other planets.

Hanging Around

Make a planet mobile to help you remember our neighbors in space. Each planet is cut from a different decorated paper. (Jupiter, Saturn, Uranus, and Neptune are all surrounded by rings, but only Saturn's — certainly the most spectacular — are shown.)

MERCURY
Bubble Painting
Paint your paper with a wash of grayish brown paint. Mix 1/4 cup (50 ml) water and 1 tablespoon (15 ml) dish washing liquid in a cup. Blow through a straw inserted in the mixture until the bubbles overflow. Lower the painted side of the paper onto the bubbles (as many times as you like).

VENUS
Crayon Resist Painting
Scribble swirling lines on the paper with a white crayon. Paint a wash of creamy yellow over the scribblings.

EARTH
Flour Paste Marbling
Note: This project calls for enamel model paint. It should be used under adult supervision. You can avoid cleaning up with turpentine by using a disposable toothpick and paper plate.

Work near a sink, as you'll need water to wash the paste off your paper. Mix 1 cup (250 ml) water with 1 cup (225 g) flour until smooth. Pour into a sturdy paper plate. With a toothpick, drop blue (plus green or tan, if you like) enamel paint on the surface, then gently swirl the colors. Cut two pieces of paper slightly smaller than the plate. Lower one piece of paper onto the surface, then carefully lift; wash the paste off. Add more drops of color to the plate; repeat with the second piece of paper.

MARS
Sand Painting
Mix red and black powdered poster paint with a small amount of clean sand. Paint your paper with slightly watered-down glue, then sprinkle the sand mixture over the surface. Tip the excess from the paper.

YOU'LL NEED

- Decorated heavyweight drawing paper (see planet names for specific materials and instructions)
- Compass (optional)
- Scissors
- Thin string
- White glue
- Dowel or straight stick

For each planet, cut two circles the same size from decorated paper. (Cut the planets to scale, if you like, although Saturn and Jupiter are huge compared to the other planets.) Glue the two circles together, wrong sides facing, with one end of a length of string sandwiched between them. Leave to dry under a heavy weight, such as a stack of books. To complete the mobile, tie the planets to the dowel, in their order from the sun.

JUPITER
Torn–Paper Collage
Tear yellow, orange, and brown tissue paper in strips of varying widths. Paste them on your paper with slightly watered-down glue.

SATURN
Mixed Media
For the planet, brush water on your paper, then paint bands of yellow and orange paint.

To make the rings, form three circles from pipe cleaners—one red, one orange, and one yellow. Cut two V-shaped notches on opposite sides of the finished planet. slightly off-center, as shown. Place the rings around Saturn, resting them in the notches.

URANUS
Salt Painting
Paint a wash of bluish-green paint over your paper. While it is wet, sprinkle salt on the paint. When the paint and paper are dry, rub off the salt crystals.

NEPTUNE
Plastic-Wrap Painting
Paint your paper with a wash of blue paint. While still wet, lay plastic wrap on top of the paint. Set aside for five minutes, then remove the plastic wrap.

PLUTO
Splatter Painting
Spread out plenty of newspaper, as this can be messy! Spatter brown, gray, and black paint on your paper by tapping the brush against the handle of another paintbrush.

HANDY HINT

Here's one clever way to recall the names of the planets in the order in which they orbit the sun. Just remember Men Very Early Made Jars Serve Useful Needs, Period.

The Whirling Wind

※

A Tale from Mexico

Swirling columns of air known as dust devils (also sand devils and dancing devils) are common in many desert regions of the world. In this spooky tale from Mexico, a boy's life is forever changed when he meets up with one of these devilish winds.

In a town somewhere in Mexico, there once lived a boy named Pablo (PAHB-low). Pablo was a likable child, who worked hard in school and was always ready to help his parents around the house. There was just one problem with Pablo. He was curious about many things, especially concerning the natural world. While curiosity is usually a good thing, Pablo's curiosity sometimes got the better of him.

Once when he was younger, he wondered what the birds could see from their perches high in the trees. To find out, he climbed up a tall tree—only to discover he couldn't make his way down by himself. Another time, Pablo was nearly knocked unconscious when he stood outdoors during a hailstorm trying to catch hailstones. "I just wondered if I could catch one," he said to his parents.

Pablo was equally intrigued by the whirlwinds that sometimes blew through his village. "Be careful, my son. Keep away from them," Pablo's father warned. "You remember the story they tell about the boy who was sucked up by such a whirlwind. He was never heard from again."

Pablo was fascinated by this tale of long ago. "Did that really ever happen, Papá?" he asked his father. "How could a person get sucked into a whirlwind and just disappear?" But his father only shrugged and said he did not know.

Maybe these stories about whirlwinds are just meant to scare us children, Pablo thought to himself. He asked his teacher what would happen if you

got sucked into a whirlwind and he asked the man who owned the village store what would happen. He even asked the oldest person in the village. They all said the same thing: Stay away from whirlwinds.

One day after school, Pablo was playing outside with his little dog, Gordito (gor-DEE-toh). The wind had started to pick up, and Pablo could see that the air was thick with dust near the old cart track that lead to the mountains. "Come on, Gordito," he urged his dog. "I'll bet we'll be able to spot some whirlwinds there."

At first, the wind just ruffled Pablo's hair and blew Gordito's ears so that they looked like flags flapping in the breeze.

Then it grew strong enough so that Pablo had to button his jacket closed and squint his eyes to keep the dust from blowing into them. "This is nothing," he said to himself. "Why is everyone so concerned about a little wind?"

But Pablo didn't see the whirling mass of air that had formed just a few yards ahead. Round and round it swirled, picking up speed, and growing in size, until it began to draw Pablo towards it like a huge magnet. Pablo began to have second thoughts about this devilish wind. He tried moving away from the swirling air. Planting his feet firmly, one after another, he staggered away from the whirlwind, calling frantically for Gordito to follow.

"Come, Gordito!" he shouted above the noise of the blowing sand. "It's time to go home!"

But Gordito was no match for the mighty wind, and it kept drawing the little dog closer and closer to it. Pablo turned and ran back for his dog, grabbing him by the collar. But the dusty cyclone swirled and sucked at them all the harder. Before they knew it, Pablo and Gordito were swallowed by the swirling air.

Inside the whirlwind, the boy and his dog were tossed about like dried chiles. Then just as abruptly, the wind stopped. Pablo and Gordito landed on the ground with a thud. The boy shakily picked himself off the ground. He rubbed his eyes and began brushing off his trousers. He stopped when he saw his hands.

His hands were like those of an old man—the fingers crooked and swollen, the skin dry and cracked. Pablo tried to straighten his back, but he could only stand stooped over like some of the old men who spent their days in the shade on the plaza. Pablo stared at Gordito. The little dog had aged terribly, too. The hair on his muzzle had turned gray, and his back sagged and his legs were stiff. Gordito wagged his tail with difficulty and looked up at Pablo with mournful eyes.

Pablo hardly knew what to think, and he had no idea what he would say to his parents when he got home. He and Gordito hobbled back towards the village. Rounding the corner of his street, Pablo stopped dead in his tracks. Where his house should have been, stood a crumbling adobe ruin. Tall weeds grew from what was left of the roof, and all the glass in the windows had been broken. The front door was battered and dangled from a single hinge.

Some small children were playing in the ruins of the house. Pablo called to them, startled by the sound of his voice. "Hey, you kids, what are you doing? Get away from my house!" he croaked.

"Your house?" jeered one of the children with a laugh. "Nobody lives in this old heap of mud! Our parents used to play here when they were kids."

Then Pablo understood what had happened. The whirlwind had robbed him of the best years of his life. Even worse, time had gone on without him. Not only had his parents died, but their neglected home had fallen into disrepair. Nothing remained of Pablo's former world save his dog, Gordito—as ravaged by time as he was.

The villagers called Pablo and Gordito "the crazy old man and his dog," because whenever a whirlwind was spotted in town, the two would chase it up one street and down another. The locals just shook their heads. They didn't know what Pablo was thinking. He was sure that if he could find the whirlwind that had stolen his youth he could regain those lost years.

The village children grew to love crazy, old Pablo. He always had a kind word for them, and they especially loved listening to his stories. "Tell us the one about the boy who got sucked up by a whirlwind!" they clamored. "Is it true this happened to someone you knew when you were a boy?"

Pablo just smiled and said nothing. He knew no one would ever believe him.

But he continued to believe the secret of his lost youth would be found in that one special whirlwind. Every day, he and Gordito waited for it. It is said the two are still waiting to this day.

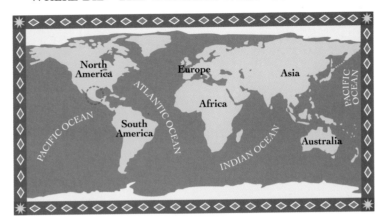

Country: MEXICO
Capital: MEXICO CITY
Continent: NORTH AMERICA
Language: SPANISH

Have You Seen the Wind?

The whirling winds that swallowed Pablo and his dog show just what a powerful force wind can be. Not surprisingly, winds are featured in stories told all over the world. Just as in this story, some of these legends describe what happens when the wind gets out of hand.

One such tale is told by the Abenaki Indians of the northeastern United States and Canada. According to the story, an enormous bird, the wind eagle, makes its home on a bald mountaintop. When the eagle flaps its wings, there is wind. When it flaps its wings harder, there is more wind, sometimes too much wind. During one of these windy spells, Gluskabi (gloo-SKAH-bee), a powerful being in Abenaki lore, is so annoyed that he climbs to the top of the mountain and ties the wings of the wind eagle to its body. Several days pass; the air is perfectly still, and it's unbearably hot. The water in the lake starts to smell, and animals and people begin to suffer. Realizing his mistake, Gluskabi climbs back up the mountain and cuts the eagle's bonds. He must admit that it's good that sometimes it's windy and sometimes it's not.

Up to Speed

Sir Francis Beaufort (BO-fort), a 19th century English admiral, noticed that he could tell how hard the wind was blowing by watching its effect on water. He devised a visual wind-speed scale (later adapted to include the effects of wind on land) that is still in use today. The scale ranges from 0 (calm) to 12 (winds of hurricane force).

You can make your own Beaufort scale to help you learn the signs associated with different wind speeds. Use the chart on the facing page to help you fill in the information on your spinning scale.

YOU'LL NEED

- 2 sheets heavyweight paper
- Drawing compass, or small plate
- Ruler
- Fine-tipped marker
- Scissors
- Paper fastener

1. Using the compass or tracing around a plate, draw a large circle on one sheet of paper. Divide the circle into 12 even segments, using the ruler to draw straight lines.

2. Number the segments from 1 to 12. (Note that 0 and 1 are combined in one segment.) Referring to the chart shown on the facing page, make a simple drawing on the widest part of each segment to illustrate the wind speed. Under each drawing, write a brief description and the wind speed in miles (or kilometers) per hour. Cut out the circle.

3. Cut out a smaller circle from the other sheet of paper. Cut a V-shape, the same size as one of the segments of the larger circle, taking care to end the cuts before you reach the very center of the circle. Position this circle on top of the larger circle, and join with a paper fastener.

Beaufort scale	MPH	KM/H
0 **CALM** Smoke rises	less than 1	less than 1
1 **LIGHT AIR** Smoke drifts	1-3	1-5
2 **LIGHT BREEZE** Leaves rustle; vanes move	4-7	6-11
3 **GENTLE BREEZE** Leaves and twigs move	8-12	12-19
4 **MODERATE BREEZE** Branches move; flags flap	13-18	20-29
5 **FRESH BREEZE** Small trees sway; whitecaps on water	19-24	30-39
6 **STRONG BREEZE** Large branches move; flags beat	25-31	40-50
7 **MODERATE GALE** Whole trees move; flags beat	32-38	51-61
8 **FRESH GALE** Twigs break; walking is difficult	39-46	62-74
9 **STRONG GALE** Signs, antennas blow down	47-54	74-87
10 **WHOLE GALE** Trees uproot	55-63	88-102
11 **STORM** Much general damage	64-72	103-121
12 **HURRICANE** Wide-spread destruction	over 73	over 122

Wind Instruments

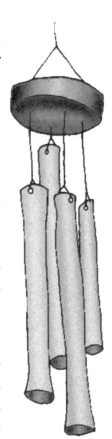

The wind rustling through the leaves creates a music all its own. You can get the wind to make a different type of music for you, as well. Hang some wind chimes outdoors, and see what kind of melody the breezes play!

Chimes can be made from all sorts of different materials, each offering its own unique sound. Hollow bamboo chimes are popular in Asian countries. They echo with a deep, wooden sound. Shapes made from baked clay can be found in such places as Italy and Mexico. Island nations make tinkling wind chimes from seashells.

You can make your own wind chimes from various materials found in the home. Tie different items with fishing line to a stick or fat dowel, positioning them close enough so that they'll touch when blown by the wind.

WINDS OF CHANGE

Long ago, people believed that special wind gods, or the earth breathing in and out, caused winds to blow. Today we know that winds are created by high-pressure and low-pressure areas.

Simply put, even though we can't feel it, the air around us has weight and therefore pressure. The air is heated by the sun, but it is heated unevenly, thanks to such features as mountains and bodies of water. As some of the air is heated, it rises. This rising causes a low-pressure area to form beneath it. Air from higher-pressure areas then drops to take its place. This exchange and movement of air is what we call wind.

High Flyer

In some parts of the world, there are only two distinct seasons—a dry season and a rainy one. Right before the rains come, the winds blow. And what are steady winds good for? For flying kites, of course!

You can make your own kite that is perfect for flying in a gentle breeze—that's 3 on the Beaufort scale, or about 8 to 12 miles (13 to 19 km) per hour. This compact kite is folded, origami-style, from paper (which is appropriate, since kite flying and paper folding are both popular pastimes originating in Asia).

YOU'LL NEED

• Several 8 ½-inch by 11-inch (21 cm by 27.5 cm) sheets of paper
• Scissors
• Tape
• Thin string

1. Fold one short end of one of the sheets of paper so that it meets the long side; crease well. Cut away the excess paper.

2. Unfold the paper. Fold two neighboring edges so that they meet along the crease line.

3. Fold back the corner of one of the flaps so that it touches the outer edge. Fold the other corner the same way. Pull up on both corners to open up the paper.

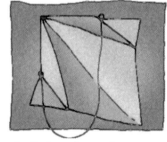

4. Cut a piece of string 24 inches (60 cm) long. Tape one end of the string to each side of the paper where the short crease lines end. This is the kite's bridle. Tie your kite string to the middle of the bridle.

5. Cut one or more of the remaining sheets of paper into thin strips. Tape several strips together to make a tail. Tape the tail to the end of the kite farthest from the bridle. (Note: If the kite repeatedly dives and spins, you may need to add to the tail. If the kite won't climb, try making the tail a little shorter.)

It's a Breeze

Cooling breezes help make the hot days of summer more bearable. Of course, the wind doesn't always blow when we want it to. So what's a hot body to do? Create a breeze — with the help of a fan!

Dozens of different fan designs are found around the world. Some are nothing more than a huge plant leaf; others, like the hand-painted silk folding fans of Japan, are true works of art. The example shown here is based on a fan design from Nigeria. It is traditionally made from leather, decorated with appliquéed (sewn on) designs.

YOU'LL NEED

- Brown cardboard
- Scissors
- Paint stirrer
- White glue
- White construction paper
- Paintbrush

1. Cut an oval shape from the cardboard, about 10 inches (16 cm) wide by 14 inches (22.5 cm) long. Glue the paint stirrer to one side of the oval. Set aside to dry.

2. Cut designs from white paper folded in half (pencil half the design along the folded edge; when unfolded, the design will be whole). Use some of the traditional Nigerian designs shown here, or invent your own.

3. Brush glue (thinned with a little water) on one side of the designs, then glue them down on the cardboard. When you have finished, brush glue over the entire front and back of the fan to protect the designs and add strength to the cardboard. Let dry completely.

The Return of the Clouds

A Tale from the Zuni Indians

*Stories about clouds (and the much-needed rain they bring) are found in
many of the drier regions of the world. This Pueblo tale, told by the Zuni Indians of
western New Mexico, describes how a resourceful boy once saved the people in his
village when he found a way to return the clouds to the sky.*

They say that a long time ago Ahaiyuta (ah-high-YOU-tah), Child of the Sun, lived with his grandmother. Like other boys his age, Ahaiyuta looked forward to the day when he would prove that he was no longer a child but a man.

That day finally arrived. Ahaiyuta's grandmother sat the boy down to explain the task he had been given.

"Child of the Sun, your test is not an easy one," the old woman said. "You must do something that no one else has ever been able to do."

"And what is that, Grandmother?" Ahaiyuta asked.

"You must find Cloud Eater and kill him so that we may have rain."

Ahaiyuta had heard many stories about Cloud Eater. Cloud Eater was a monster as tall as a mountain peak, with an enormous appetite for clouds. Sometimes Cloud Eater succeeded in devouring every cloud in the sky for months on end. No clouds meant no rain, and no rain meant certain death for plants, animals… and people.

Cloud Eater had been at it again. The corn in the fields had turned brown and shriveled up. Animals were little more than skin and bones. The ground was so dry it had turned to dust. Brave men had been sent to find Cloud Eater and destroy him, and they had traveled far and wide, but all in vain. No one could even discover where the monster lived.

"You may have better luck, my grandson," said Ahaiyuta's grandmother. "Anyway, here are some feathers to help you." And the old woman handed Ahaiyuta four feathers—one red, one blue, one yellow, and one black.

"The red feather will help guide you to Cloud Eater," the boy's grandmother explained. "All you have to do is put it in your hair, and it will steer you in the right direction. Stick the blue feather in your hair, and you will be able to talk with the animals. The yellow feather has a special medicine, too. With it, you can shrink in size."

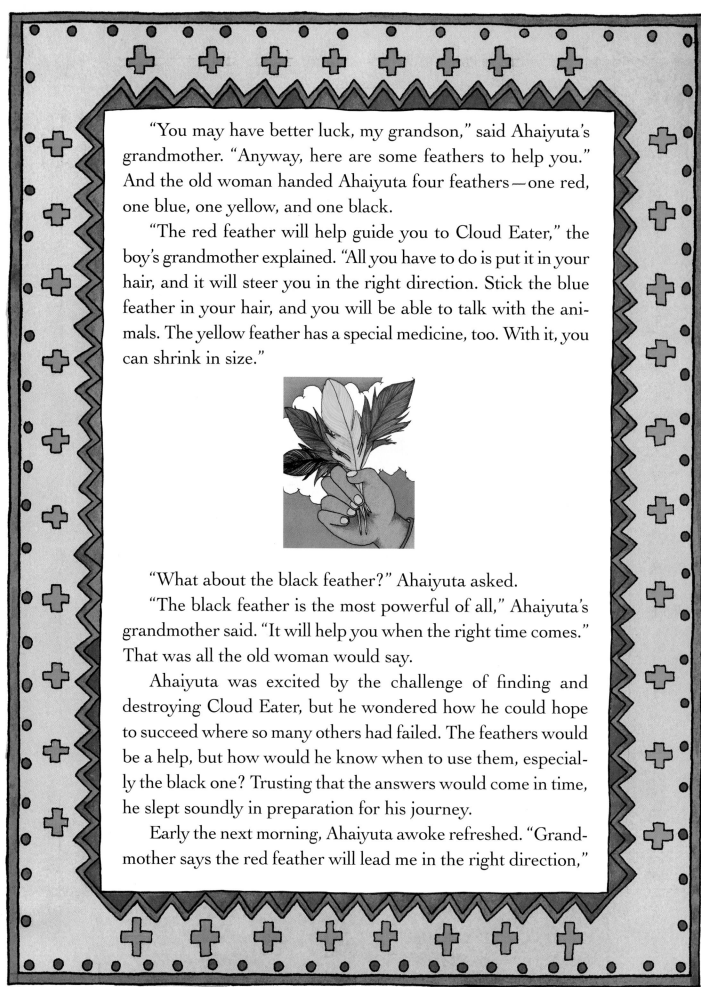

"What about the black feather?" Ahaiyuta asked.

"The black feather is the most powerful of all," Ahaiyuta's grandmother said. "It will help you when the right time comes." That was all the old woman would say.

Ahaiyuta was excited by the challenge of finding and destroying Cloud Eater, but he wondered how he could hope to succeed where so many others had failed. The feathers would be a help, but how would he know when to use them, especially the black one? Trusting that the answers would come in time, he slept soundly in preparation for his journey.

Early the next morning, Ahaiyuta awoke refreshed. "Grandmother says the red feather will lead me in the right direction," he said to himself, sticking the feather in his hair. He spun around in place, to clear the air and let the feather's magic take over. When he came to a complete stop, he set off in the direction the feather indicated.

Ahaiyuta walked all day, stopping only occasionally to eat and drink. His feet were sore and his legs seemed to grow heavier with every step, but he pushed on. Ahaiyuta noticed that it was getting hotter and hotter. There were fewer trees, and these gradually gave way to scrubby bushes. Before long, there was little more than a few clumps of dried grass dotting the ground. Oddly, there was no sign of any animals at all.

So Ahaiyuta couldn't help but jump back in surprise when a few yards ahead of him a mole popped its head up from an opening in the ground.

Thinking quickly, Ahaiyuta slipped the blue feather in his hair, and bent down to speak to the tiny animal.

"Good day, Lone Mole. I am trying to find Cloud Eater. Can you tell me where he lives?"

"You are headed in the right direction," replied Mole, "but Cloud Eater's home is four days' journey from here. How ever did you know to come this way?"

"It's a long story," replied Ahaiyuta.

"Well, it's much too hot for stories," said Mole. "And it's much too hot up here," he added, turning to retreat underground.

"Then let me join you in your tunnel," Ahaiyuta said.

Mole looked quizzically at the boy. "You're much too big," he said.

"Not now," said Ahaiyuta, with a laugh, sticking the yellow feather in his hair and gradually shrinking until he was eye-level with the mole.

Following the animal into an underground chamber, Ahaiyuta told him why he was looking for Cloud Eater. "Things are no better around here," Mole told the boy. "Cloud Eater has taken to eating more than just clouds. Lately he's been gobbling up

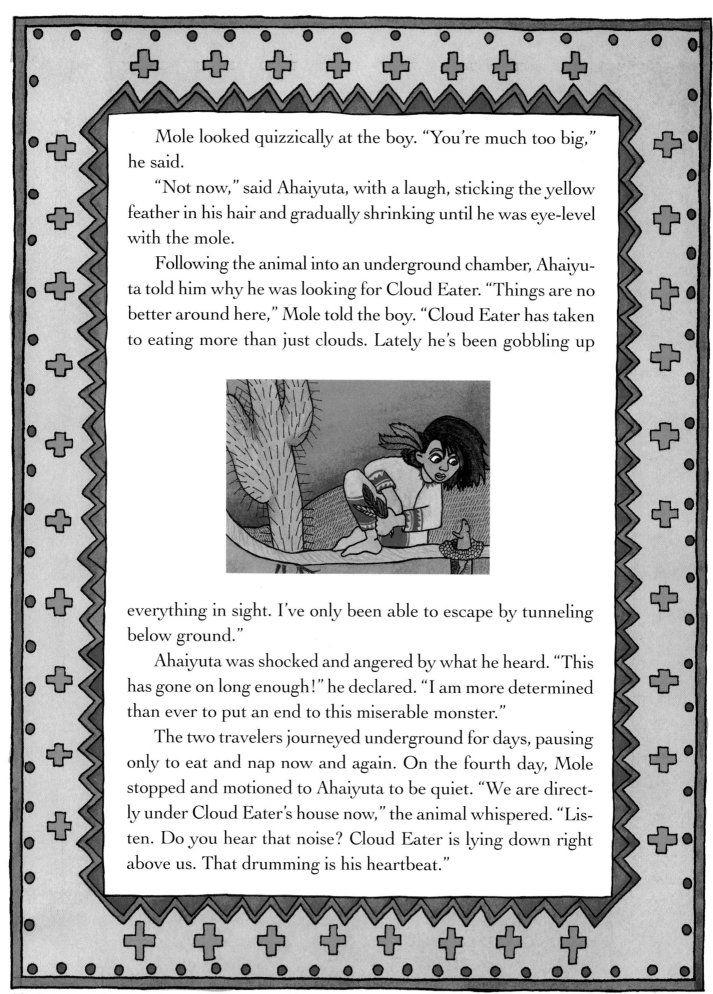

everything in sight. I've only been able to escape by tunneling below ground."

Ahaiyuta was shocked and angered by what he heard. "This has gone on long enough!" he declared. "I am more determined than ever to put an end to this miserable monster."

The two travelers journeyed underground for days, pausing only to eat and nap now and again. On the fourth day, Mole stopped and motioned to Ahaiyuta to be quiet. "We are directly under Cloud Eater's house now," the animal whispered. "Listen. Do you hear that noise? Cloud Eater is lying down right above us. That drumming is his heartbeat."

Ahaiyuta hesitated, unsure just what he should do. Then he remembered the black feather and its powerful medicine. "I hope the right time has come!" he said, sticking the feather in his hair.

Taking care not to make a sound, Ahaiyuta drew a slingshot from his pouch and positioned a tiny rock in its cradle. He knelt down on one knee and stretched his arms out high above his head. Pulling back the sling as far as it would go, Ahaiyuta loosed the rock with a tremendous twang.

All at once there was a roar and a rumble, and the ground began to shake and a shower of rocks and dirt came thundering down. Ahaiyuta was knocked flat by the avalanche. The next thing he knew he was propped up on his elbows, staring at the outstretched body of Cloud Eater.

"You did it!" shouted Mole triumphantly when he saw Ahaiyuta was awake. "You killed Cloud Eater! Now that he is dead, we shall have rain!"

"But I don't remember anything after I shot the pebble through the ground," the boy remarked. "What happened?"

"Your aim was perfect," Mole said. "You struck Cloud Eater right in the heart. When you hit him, he rolled over, collapsing the roof of our tunnel. I dug through the rubble and pulled you out."

"Thank you for saving my life," Ahaiyuta said. "And thank you for saving my people. We are finally rid of Cloud Eater." Turning to gaze at the huge clouds that were already forming in the sky, he shouted, "Look, here come the clouds! Let it rain! Let it pour!"

And that is the end of the story, the story of Ahaiyuta and how he brought back the clouds on his way to becoming a man.

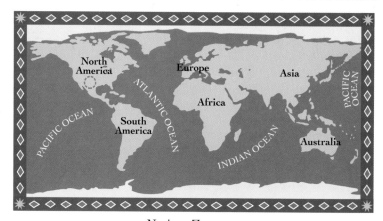

Nation: Zuni
Region: Western
New Mexico
Continent: North America
Language: Tanoan

In the Clouds

In the ancient world, clouds were commonly associated with the storm gods of the heavens. Sometimes, they were regarded as clothing for the dieties. The sky god of the Skidi Pawnee, Native Americans who lived in what is modern-day Nebraska, supposedly wore such a cloud garment. When he spread his arms, the clouds stretched across the entire length of the sky.

In other parts of the world, clouds were evidence of the dust or water that was churned up by fearsome creatures roaming the heavens. Some of these monsters were believed to stand guard over clouds, preventing rain from falling. During dry spells in India, people cheered on a storm god who battled an enormous dragon that ruled the heavens. Only if the storm god succeeded in diverting the dragon's attention away from the clouds did it rain.

Cloud Cover

The daytime sky is like an ever-changing artist's canvas. One minute it's dotted with tiny white clouds, the next it's streaked with gray. There may be clouds blanketing the entire sky, or just one or two hovering over a lake or lone mountaintop. Often there are two, or even more, types of clouds in the sky at the same time.

In 1803, an English scientist named Luke Howard came up with the system of classifying the different cloud shapes, one that is still in use today. The ten basic types, and their usual place in the sky, are illustrated below.

How can anyone ever keep the names straight? It's easy if you know what the different parts of the cloud names mean. The following three terms describe the three main shapes of clouds:

Cirrus (SEER-us) clouds are curly.
Cumulus (QUOOM-yoo-lus) clouds are puffy.
Stratus (STRA-tus) clouds are layered.

It's also helpful to know that:
Cirro is used as a prefix for very high clouds.
Alto is the prefix for middle-level clouds.
Nimbus (sometimes written as nimbo) means "rain cloud."

Cirrocumulus clouds, then, are high, puffy clouds, and nimbostratus are layered rain clouds. Now see if you can identify the clouds that are in the sky today!

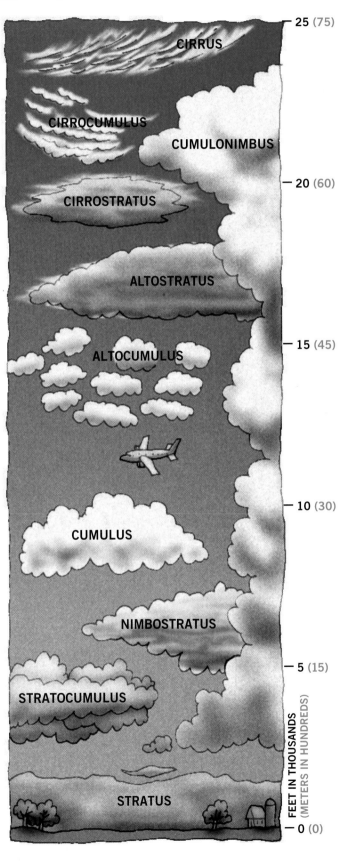

Bottled Up

On a cold day, you can see your breath. Did you know that each breath is actually a cloud? It's true! When the warm air you breathe out of your nose and mouth meets the cold surrounding air, it quickly condenses and forms a miniature, short-lived cloud.

You don't need a cold day to do another simple experiment that demonstrates how clouds form. You will need an adult to light the candle, however.

YOU'LL NEED

- Large, clear glass jug or bottle with a narrow opening
- Candle and matches

1. Have an adult light the candle. Turn the glass jug upside down and hold it over the flame for about 5 seconds. Blow out the candle.

2. Let the glass cool, then wipe the jug mouth with a tissue (to remove any soot on the edge). Put your mouth over the jug opening so that it is covered completely. Blow hard into the jug. Watch to see what happens in the jug when you remove your mouth.

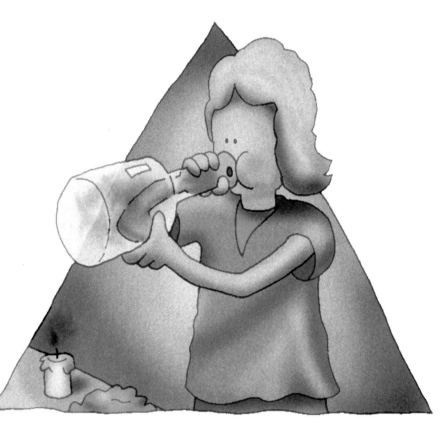

WHAT'S HAPPENING?

What was that swirling mass in the jug that looked like a cloud? It was a cloud! But how did you make it form?

First off, you filled the air in the bottle with soot from the burning wick. There is similar soot in air all around us—everything from dust and pollen to pollution.

Second, you added warm, moist air from your breath. The air around us is also full of moisture, due to evaporation from rivers, lakes, and oceans.

But the cloud only formed when you removed your mouth, which made the air in the jug cool suddenly.

The same thing happens in the sky. When air cools, some of the moisture in the air condenses, forming tiny water droplets. They cling to the soot particles. And that's what a cloud is: a mass of millions of microscopic water droplets.

Scattered Clouds

A cloud-filled sky on a windy day is quite a sight. All sorts of fantastic pictures take shape as the clouds stream across the sky.

You and your friends can send some clouds racing right here on solid ground. This race is an adaptation of a popular game played by children throughout Britain. They call it Kippers (because the shapes they cut from paper are fish). You'll call it fun!

YOU'LL NEED

- White poster board
- Scissors
- Newspaper

VARIATIONS ON A THEME

As "The Return of the Clouds" makes clear, there can't be rain without clouds. But there can be clouds without rain. When the sky is dotted with small puffy clouds, it will stay pleasant for the foreseeable future. Wispy clouds high in the sky are also usually indicators of fair weather.

1. Have each contestant cut a fat cloud shape from the poster board. The clouds should be about the same size, to make it fair. Each player also gets a double sheet of newspaper to create the "wind."

2. Mark both a starting line and a finish line. Have the players lay their clouds on the starting line. Using the newspaper to fan the air (players may roll or fold the sheet however they like), have the players move their clouds toward the end. The first one across the finish line is the winner.

On Cloud Nine

While you can't nap in the clouds, you can do the next best thing—rest your head on a pillow that's as soft as a cloud!

This pillow has a little something extra to make your slumbers special. It has a pocket that holds a small sachet (sa-SHAY), or packet, of dried herbs. Fill yours with sweet-smelling lavender or dried rose petals, or try something a little different, such as dill seeds (once used by Scandinavians to lull babies to sleep). Happy dreams!

YOU'LL NEED

- ½ yard (.5 m) white cotton fabric
- Ruler
- Scissors
- Fabric paints
- Needle and thread
- Stuffing
- Dried herbs or spices

1. Fold the fabric in half, and draw a fluffy cloud shape on one side. Add a ½-inch (1.25 cm) seam allowance all around. Cut out the cloud shape (you will have two identical pieces). Measure and cut out three small square pieces (remember to add extra for seam allowances) for the herb pocket and sachet.

2. Turn in the seam allowances on one square and pin it to one of the cloud pieces. Stitch around three sides with small, even stitches (by hand or with a sewing machine). Decorate one or both sides of the pillow with the fabric paint. Copy the designs shown here, or create your own. Set the paint according to the manufacturer's directions.

Extra! Extra!

"On cloud nine" is an expression used to describe someone who is extremely happy. Clouds figure in other well-known words and sayings, such as "cloud-burst" or "with one's head in the clouds." Use these and other colorful cloud expressions in a game of Charades. (For another version of this game, see "Sunny Side Up" on page 31.)

In the clouds

Cloud-cuckoo-land

Cloudberry

Cloudy

Cloud cover

Cloudscape

With a chance of clouds

Under a cloud

3. With the right sides facing, sew the pillow pieces together, leaving an opening for the stuffing. Clip the seam allowances, then turn the pillow right-side out, and lightly stuff. Sew the opening shut by hand.

4. Make the sachet by sewing the remaining fabric squares together on three sides. Turn the fabric right-side out, and fill with dried herbs or potpourri (a mixture of dried flowers, herbs, and spices). Sew the opening shut. Place the sachet in the pillow pocket (be sure to remove it before launder-ing the pillow).

After the Rain

✳

A Tale from Kenya

As storm clouds move across the sky, they sometimes leave behind a pleasant surprise. The shimmering rainbow is certainly one of nature's most spectacular offerings. This tale from Kenya, a country located in East Africa, explains just how the rainbow comes to be in the sky.

Once, a long, long time ago, Mkunga Mburu (mah-KOON-gah mah-BOO-roo), the god of thunder, did not visit this land for many months. "Where is Mkunga Mburu and his mighty bullock?" the people asked. They knew the thunder god traveled the heavens on a huge black bull, with a spear in each hand ready to hurl at the clouds. "How much longer must we wait before he pierces the clouds and brings us rain?"

The village chieftain could not tell his people when Mkunga Mburu would arrive. "I can only tell you what our grandfathers did when the thunder god stayed away," the old chieftain said.

"What did they do?" the people wanted to know.

"The people all stood together and shouted in one voice," the chieftain replied.

"What did they shout?" the people wanted to know.

"Our grandfathers shouted 'Mkunga Mburu, can you hear us? We have been without rain for too long. Bring us rain, Mkunga Mburu. Please, bring us rain!'" This the chieftain told his people.

"Then we should try that," the people said.

That afternoon the people assembled in front of the chieftain's hut. Together they shouted, "Mkunga Mburu, can you hear us? We have been without rain for too long. Bring us rain, Mkunga Mburu. Please, bring us rain!"

"We have done it," the chieftain said. "All we can do is wait."

The people waited, but by the next day the rain had still not come. They

decided to shout for Mkunga Mburu again. "Mkunga Mburu, can you hear us? We have been without rain for too long. Bring us rain, Mkunga Mburu. Please, bring us rain!" the people called out.

The people waited another day, and when it still had not rained, they cried out to Mkunga Mburu once again. "Hear us, mighty one!" they pleaded.

That afternoon, the villagers grew excited. "Aren't those the hoofbeats of Mkunga Mburu's bull thundering in the distance?" The people looked up and saw the great black body of Mkunga Mburu's bull slowly galloping toward them, flanked by swirling gray clouds. "The bull's hooves raise a lot of dust," the people said. Now and again great flashes of lightning electrified the sky. "Look, those are the metal tips of the thunder god's spears."

At long last, the clouds gathered above the village and the rain began to fall. The villagers clapped their hands and shouted their thanks to the thunder god.

Mkunga Mburu looked down from the heavens and smiled. "The rain is making the people happy," he thought to himself. "That is good. I can make the people even happier. I shall give them more rain."

Mkunga Mburu urged his great beast on. Back and forth across the sky the thunder god rode, thrusting his spears into the clouds at every chance. The sky boomed and flashed, and the rain continued to fall.

And fall, and fall. It rained for many days, and the village people began to worry.

"First we had too little rain and the crops withered and died. Now we have too much rain and the crops are drowning."

The people decided to summon Mkunga Mburu once again, only this time to ask him to please stop the rain. They gathered in front of the chieftain's hut and cried out in one voice, "It is enough, Mkunga Mburu. Thank you, but it is enough!"

Mkunga Mburu heard the people's cry. He looked down and

saw the flooded fields and rain-soaked huts. Turning his bull quickly, he dug his heels into its sides. The booming of the bullock's hooves grew faint as the great god and his mighty beast lumbered away.

Behind the people, the clouds parted, revealing the smiling face of the sun. The people smiled back at the sun, then turned to bid farewell to the departing thunder god. Stretching across the sky in front of them was a bright ribbon of red, yellow, green, blue, and violet.

"Look!" the people shouted, pointing at the shimmering rainbow. "What is that?"

"Mkunga Mburu must have dropped his robe as he was leaving," said the chieftain.

So he had. And just as in times past, the hem of Mkunga Mburu's robe is sometimes visible in the sky, after the rain.

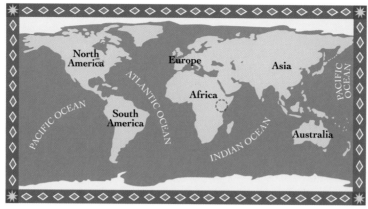

Country: KENYA
Capital: NAIROBI
Continent: AFRICA
Languages: SWAHILI, ENGLISH

Spanning the Sky

Just imagine how our distant ancestors reacted when they looked up after a rain and noticed a band of colors arched across the sky. Not surprisingly, in many cultures, the rainbow was thought to be something belonging to the storm or thunder god. Often it was an article of clothing (like Mkunga Mburu's robe in the story), or a weapon, such as a bow. That's where we get the name rainbow.

Many peoples, including some South American tribes and the Aborigines of Australia, describe the rainbow as a colorful serpent that stretches its length from one end of the sky to the other. Other cultures see the rainbow as a bridge connecting heaven and earth. The Wyandot Indians said that the first animals came from the heavens by way of such a bridge.

While seeing a rainbow brings a person luck according to European tradition (lucky indeed is the person who finds the pot of gold at its end!), in some places rainbows are viewed with suspicion. Like other rare natural occurrences, they are considered bad omens. The San people of southern Africa tell a tale about a horrible rainbow fire, which is why whenever a rainbow is spotted, San children strike sticks together to scare it away.

Nature's Color Wheel

Just as in the story, real-life rainbows appear after a rain. At least the rain needs to have stopped where you are—it actually needs to be falling in another part of the sky. That's because rainbows are formed when sunlight hits these distant raindrops, bending and bouncing off them in such a way that we see the resulting bands of color.

Just what are those colors? Starting at the outer curve of the rainbow's arch, they are red, orange, yellow, green, blue, indigo (a dark blue), and violet. If a second rainbow is visible, its colors are fainter and reversed.

ROUND AND ROUND

The arching rainbow we see is actually just a portion of a complete circle. (From an airplane, under the right conditions, you can see the full circle—quite a sight!) The portion of the circle we see depends on the sun's position in the sky. When the sun is low on the horizon, rainbows arch high in the sky. When the sun is overhead, rainbows are closer to the ground.

Across the Spectrum

R
O
Y
G.

HELPFUL HINTS

Here's an easy way to remember the order of the colors of the rainbow. Just think of ROY G. BIV, and you have the first initials of the seven colors of the rainbow in proper order.

In nature, the conditions must be just right for a rainbow to form. In your backyard, you can create one rainbow after another with little more than a garden hose.

Just as in nature, you need sunlight to pull off this trick. Early morning or late afternoon is best, when the sun is lower in the sky. Standing with your back to the sun, spray the water in a fine mist so that it arches in front of you. Move slowly until you can see the miniature rainbow in the water spray. Can you make out the spectrum of colors?

You can also create a rainbow indoors (no, not with a hose!) Find a sunny window with a ledge. Place a glass of water—filled to the very top—on the ledge, so that it extends over the edge slightly. You'll notice a tiny rainbow projected on the floor. Place a piece of white paper under the image to make the colors show up even more clearly.

Wearing the Rainbow

The Shoshoni Indians of the western United States regarded the rainbow as a snake. They tell a story of how this brightly-colored reptile once helped them during a terrible drought. While the people watched, Rainbow Snake jumped into the sky, stretching and growing to an enormous size. It used its scales to scrape ice from the clouds, which melted from the warmth of the sun and fell as rain.

Model a colorful clay necklace shaped like a serpent in honor of Rainbow Snake. Be sure to ask for an adult's help when using the oven.

YOU'LL NEED

- Oven-hardening polymer clay, in bright red, dark blue, yellow, and white
- Nail
- Embroidery floss or thin string

1. Mix small batches of clay in the seven colors of the rainbow.
RED—red
ORANGE—red and yellow
YELLOW—yellow
GREEN—yellow and dark blue (add white for a lighter shade, if desired)
BLUE—dark blue and white
INDIGO—dark blue
VIOLET—red, dark blue, and white

2. To make the necklace shown, mold a snake head from red clay, adding features, such as eyes, with tiny bits of other colors. Form six to ten beads in each of the seven colors. Last, shape a tapering tail from violet clay. Pierce holes in all the beads with the nail, remembering the clay will shrink slightly in the oven.

3. Bake the clay in the oven, following the manufacturer's instructions. Let the beads cool completely. String the necklace, positioning the beads so that the serpent's head and tail meet and hang in the middle of the necklace, as shown.

Colorful Coils

European folklore has it that a pot of gold awaits anyone who can find the end of the rainbow.

Maybe a different sort of container can be found there, such as the rainbow-hued basket shown here.

YOU'LL NEED

- 5 yards (5.5 m) of 5/32-inch (4-mm) cotton cord or thin clothesline
- Multicolored yarn or cotton string
- Scissors
- Tapestry needle, with a large eye

CULTURAL CLUES

Some cultures view colors in a different light. For example, in many European countries, white is a color associated with freshness, cleanliness, and purity. Bridal gowns are white; so are baby diapers and laundry powders. But in India white is considered an unlucky color, while in China it is the color of mourning.

The same is true for some of the other colors. Ask your friends from other cultures to tell you what they know about the meanings behind some of your favorite colors.

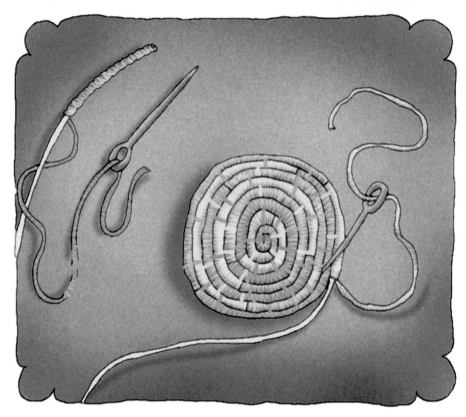

1. Cut a 4-foot (1.20 m) length of yarn and thread the tapestry needle. Do not double the yarn, or tie a knot in its end. Starting with the end of the yarn farthest from the needle, wrap 2 inches (5 cm) of the cord (starting at the very end) tightly and evenly with the yarn. Bend the wrapped portion of the cord into a tight spiral. Secure the coils by sewing the outer coil to the one just inside it, inserting the needle on the far side of the inner coil and pulling the yarn taut.

2. Put down the needle, and continue wrapping the outer coil where you left off; holding the unwrapped portion of the cord in one hand, wrap with the other. After wrapping about 1 inch (2.5 cm) of cord, you should stop and sew that portion of the coil to its inner neighbor.

Mood Indigo

Name a color and chances are you associate it with certain images. How about purple? Most likely, kings and queens come to mind. Green? This is the color of environmental conservation. You can be "green" by recycling your garbage and cutting back on wasteful consumption of gasoline and electricity.

We even describe various emotions with colors, such as "feeling blue" or "seeing red" (this is one way to say you're angry).

Because colors are rich with symbolism, they make good topics for poems. You needn't limit yourself to the colors of the rainbow, of course. What kind of poem might you write about silver or black or chartreuse (shar-TROOZ), a pale yellowy-green? The silly poem below will get you started thinking about some of the possibilities.

Ode to My Classroom Walls

I've never seen
This sickly green
Anywhere but my school.

Who knows if I'd think
Better with pink?
Wouldn't that be totally cool!

3. Continue wrapping and coiling the cord (cutting and tying on new pieces of yarn as needed), until you have made a circle about 4 inches (10 cm) in diameter. Now start building up the sides of the basket by slightly overlapping the coils as you sew them together. When the basket is the desired size, cut the cord and wrap the very end. Sew it securely to the coil beneath it before trimming the very end of the yarn.

The Theft of Thor's Hammer

A Tale from Scandinavia

The following tale from Scandinavia features some of the gods from Norse mythology, including Thor, the god of thunder. Like storm gods in other cultures, Thor was believed to be responsible for creating the awesome sound and light show otherwise known as a thunderstorm.

Listen—do you hear that rumbling overhead? It's only Thor (toor). That thundering sound is the clank and clamor of his chariot moving across the heavens. And those flashes of lightning? Those are the sparks of his mighty hammer, Mjollnir (mee-OHL-neer), crackling as it flies through the air.

Things were a lot quieter in Asgard (AHS-gard), home of Thor and the other gods, the time Mjollnir was stolen. When Thor discovered his trusted mallet missing, he was shattered. And when he learned it had been taken by Thrym (trim), lord of the treacherous frost giants, he was downright furious.

"Coward! Thieving coward!" Thor said of his archenemy. "If that no-good, lumbering iceberg thinks he can get away with this, he's sadly mistaken!"

But Thrym had only one thing in mind when he stole Mjollnir—using the hammer as a bargaining tool. For Thrym had long had his heart set on marrying Freya (FRY-ah), the flaxen-haired goddess of love. He sent word to Asgard that he was willing to return Mjollnir—in exchange for Freya's hand in marriage.

That night in the Great Hall, the gods discussed Thrym's proposal. "It's nice to know we can get your hammer back, Thor," said Frey (fry), Freya's twin brother, "but I can't say I think much of how it will be done."

"Curse the barbarian for tricking us this way!" exclaimed Odin, Thor's father. "But what are we to do? We are much too vulnerable without Mjollnir. And Mjollnir is an even more dangerous weapon in Thrym's hands."

After lengthy discussion, it was agreed that Freya would have to wed the frost giant in order to assure Mjollnir's return.

Freya, however, would have nothing to do with this plan. "If you think I would even consider marrying that coldhearted brute, you'd better think again," she announced to the others.

"But it's the only way to get Mjollnir back," Thor argued.

"You'll have to work something else out," Freya answered flatly.

Loki (LOO-keh), the son of giants who lived among the gods in Asgard, cleared his throat. The others turned in his direction, cautiously but with curiosity. While Loki was often troublesome, he was also very clever, so they were ready to listen to what he had to say.

"We can't blame Freya for not wanting to marry Thrym, but it looks as if we have no choice.

I can think of only one way to get around this. We'll trick the great oaf into thinking he's marrying Freya."

"But how can we do that?" Thor asked.

"We'll disguise you as Freya," Loki replied. Thor looked at him with disbelief. "You'll have to go through with the wedding and all, but as soon as you get the chance, you can grab Mjollnir and escape."

The gods could think of no other way to get Mjollnir back, and even Thor reluctantly agreed it was worth a chance. They sent word to Thrym that Freya was willing to marry him.

The wedding was planned for the following month. That gave the gods plenty of time to ready Thor for the momentous day. He was measured from head to toe, and seamstresses began work on a suitable wedding dress—large enough for his imposing frame. A dozen women, stitching day and night, embroidered an enormous veil, behind which Thor's red beard and hair would be hidden.

It was decided that Loki would accompany Thor to the land of the frost giants. On the fateful day, Thor was having serious misgivings about the whole idea, but Loki convinced him it would all work out in the end. "Don't worry," he said. "I'll be there to help you."

Thrym met Thor and Loki at the door to his great ice abode, delighted to find himself face to face with his future wife. "My dear, I hope you are not wearied by your journey," he said. Thor, embarrassed by the whole charade, rolled his eyes—the only part of him visible behind the yards of fabric.

Loki answered before Thor had a chance to give himself away. "Freya's just fine, I assure you. She's been talking about the wedding so much these last few days that she's lost her voice!"

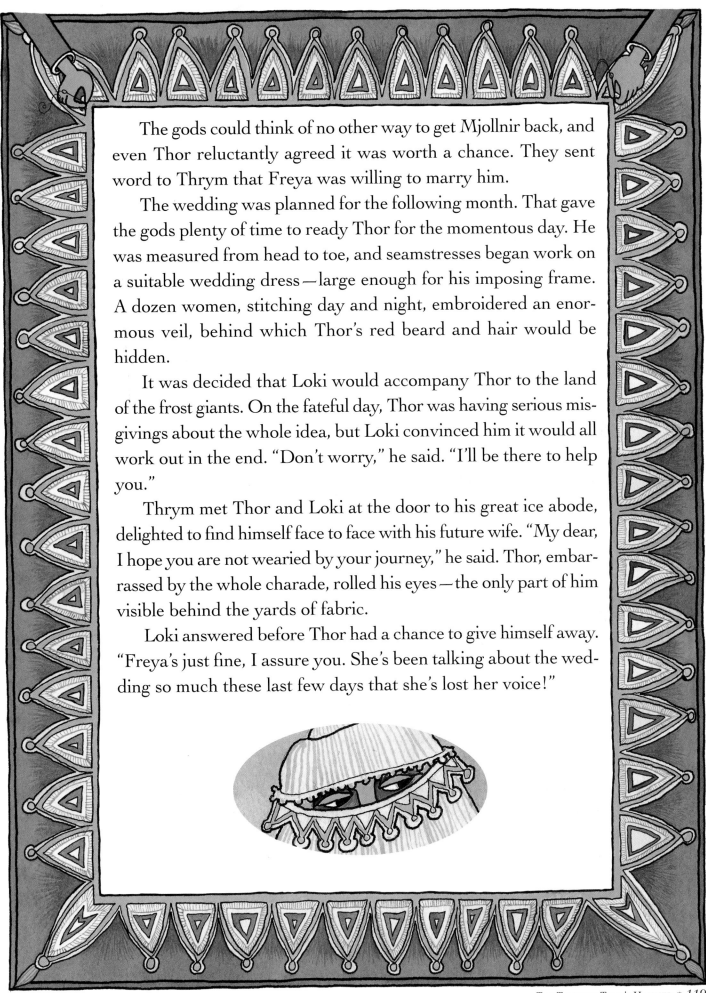

"Is that so?" chortled the frost giant. "Ho, ho! I've been so excited myself that I've hardly slept a wink for weeks!"

The marriage ceremony was brief. Thor remembered to keep his hand limp when Thrym reached for it and gave it a squeeze.

The thunder god was also careful to keep his eyes demurely lowered, thereby avoiding the frost giant's loving glances. Luckily, in the banquet hall where the wedding feast was held, the two were seated side by side.

The food was sumptuous and plentiful. The first course was soup. Thrym watched as his new bride downed not just one but three bowls of steaming soup. The frost giant's eyebrows went up, but he continued slurping his own soup in silence. Then Thor devoured a dozen soft rolls, popping them into his mouth like grapes. Thrym shook his head in wonder but still said nothing.

The main course was brought out. Thor chomped his way through half a suckling pig and nearly a whole roast lamb. Then draining a flagon of mead in a single mighty gulp, the god wiped his mouth with the back of his hand and let out a tremendous belch. Unable to contain his surprise, Thrym's jaw fell open.

Luckily, Loki noticed the frost giant's reaction, and thinking quickly, said, "Freya has been fasting for the last nine days. She's certainly worked up an appetite, wouldn't you say?"

"Har, har!" roared the frost giant. "So that is it! I was beginning to wonder if I could afford to keep my new wife!"

The volume of food and drink Thor consumed began to take its toll on the mighty god. Beads of sweat formed on his forehead, and his eyes were bloodshot and bulging in their sockets.

"Dearest," said Thrym, turning to his bride. "You don't look well. Your eyes. . . well, your eyes are looking a little. . ."

Loki jumped in once again. "Freya hasn't slept much these last few days. Nothing a good night's sleep won't fix!"

Thrym nodded uncertainly, in part because he was beginning to suspect something was not quite right with his bride, but also because he'd drunk more than his share of mead. "The excitement is catching up with me, too," he said with a yawn. Closing his eyes, the giant let his head fall back against his chair and began to snore.

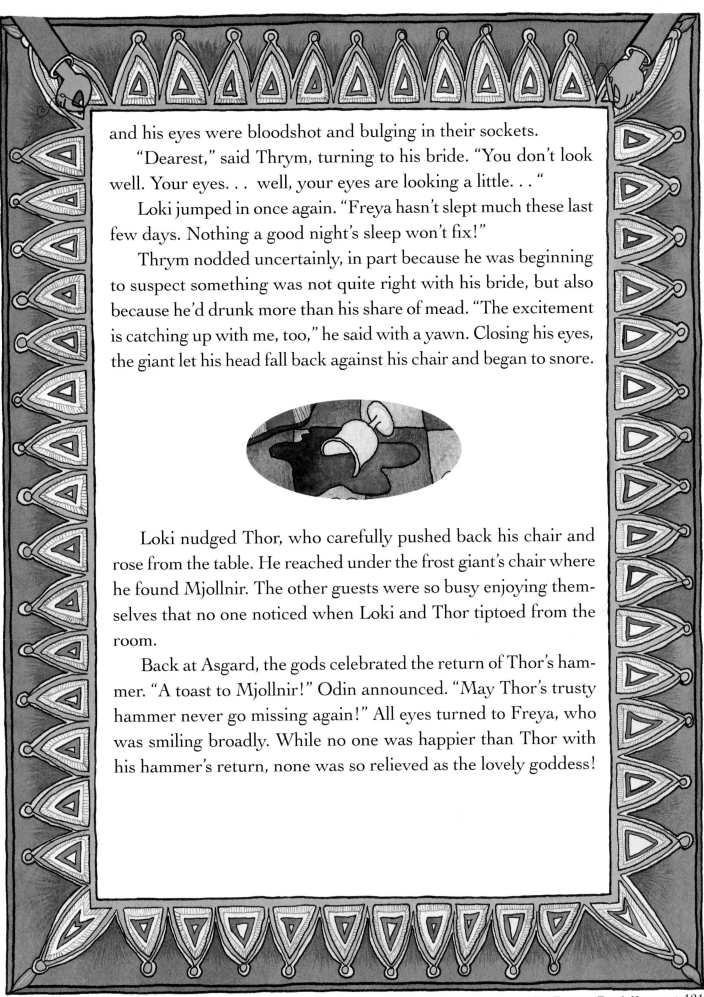

Loki nudged Thor, who carefully pushed back his chair and rose from the table. He reached under the frost giant's chair where he found Mjollnir. The other guests were so busy enjoying themselves that no one noticed when Loki and Thor tiptoed from the room.

Back at Asgard, the gods celebrated the return of Thor's hammer. "A toast to Mjollnir!" Odin announced. "May Thor's trusty hammer never go missing again!" All eyes turned to Freya, who was smiling broadly. While no one was happier than Thor with his hammer's return, none was so relieved as the lovely goddess!

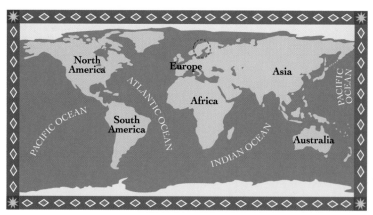

Region: SCANDINAVIA
Continent: EUROPE
Language: NORSE

Stormy Weather

Not surprisingly, many cultures around the world imagined that thunder and lightning were caused by the gods in the heavens.

Most ancient peoples thought the gods were showing their displeasure during a storm. They imagined these unseen gods hurling sharp spears and heavy hammers and axes to the ground in anger. The people down on earth considered all the light and noise a warning; when lightning actually struck, resulting in death or destruction, the people were convinced they were being punished for their wrongdoings.

The Yoruba people of Nigeria say there was a time when the storm spirit could control the people on earth with little more than thunder. Eventually the noise was not enough to make the people behave, so the storm spirit requested a more powerful magic. He was given a red powder which he spread on his tongue. From then on, whenever the storm spirit needed to scold the people, fiery lightning shot from his mouth.

Crash! Boom! Bang!

What exactly is lightning, and how is it created? While scientists are still seeking answers to all their questions, we know a lot more about storms than our distant ancestors did.

The dark, billowing clouds that form during a thunderstorm have within them both positive and negative electrical charges. Lightning occurs when there is an imbalance of charges. In an attempt to restore that balance, one charged area will "seek" an area of the opposite charge. When the attraction is so great that it overcomes normal air resistance, an electrical current begins to flow. The finale is a brilliant flash of light, as a (usually) positive charge surges upward in response (we call this flash the return stroke). This can happen within a cloud, from one cloud to another, or from a cloud to the ground.

After the flash comes a distinct crack, loud clap, or gentle rumbling—the noise we call thunder. The noise is caused by the explosive expansion of air along the lightning stroke.

Why do many seconds sometimes pass between the time we see the flash of light and the sound of the thunder? Because light travels at 186,000 miles (300,000 km) per second, we can see lightning the very instant it strikes. But sound travels more slowly, at about 1100 feet (330 m) per second, taking longer to reach our ears.

ONE MISSISSIPPI, TWO MISSISSIPPI...

A simple trick can help you estimate just how far away lightning is. Count the number of seconds between the time you see the flash of lightning and hear the thunderous boom. Divide that number by 5. This will give you the approximate distance of the strike, in miles. (If you use the metric system, convert the miles to kilometers.)

All Hands on Deck

STORM ALERT!

When storm clouds threaten, play it safe. Seek adequate shelter before the storm is upon you, and remember the following basic safety precautions. Your life may depend on it.

OUTDOORS: *Avoid taking shelter under tall trees, in small buildings that stand on their own, or anywhere in or near water. If you are the tallest object on a hill, lie flat on the ground. If the only available shelter is a car, it's best to keep your hands away from any metal parts.*

INDOORS: *Stay away from water (don't bathe or even draw water from a faucet), and don't touch any electrical appliances or the telephone. Avoid standing near windows, which might break during the storm.*

Give your reflexes a workout with a game of Lightning! This fast-paced card game for two players will fast become a favorite. Here's how to play:

Remove the Jokers from a deck of cards; shuffle well. Deal 19 cards to each player, then place two draw piles of six cards each face down on the table. Place two cards face up between the draw piles.

On the count of three, each player places four cards from his hand face-up in front of him. Working quickly and at the same time, the players try to get rid of these cards by placing them on top of the two cards in the center of the table, *in sequential order.* A Ten, for example, can be topped by a Nine or a Jack; a King by a Queen or an Ace, and so on.

As a player's upturned cards are used, more are put down from his hand. Never more than four cards may be face up (with the exception of cards of the exact same numbers, which may be stacked on top of one another).

If neither player can play any cards, both players simultaneously turn up one card each from the draw piles. If the draw piles are depleted, the players turn over the cards in the two center piles and draw from them. The first player to get rid of all the cards in his hand is the winner.

If I Had a Hammer

Hammers were associated with thunder and lightning in many parts of the ancient world. A stone carving from the 9th century B.C. shows the Hittite weather god with a hammer in one hand and a fistful of lightning bolts in the other. Ukko, the Finnish god of thunder, also wielded a heavy hammer, as did the Chinese storm god.

While you won't be able to bring on any storms with a hammer, you can use the tool to build something from wood. These handy bookends decorated with thunderbolts will be a constant reminder of the hammer's role in weathermaking!

YOU'LL NEED

- Scrap wood, such as a 1 x 6-inch pine board
- Saw
- Small finish nails
- Hammer
- Sandpaper
- Housepaint or acrylic paints
- Paintbrush

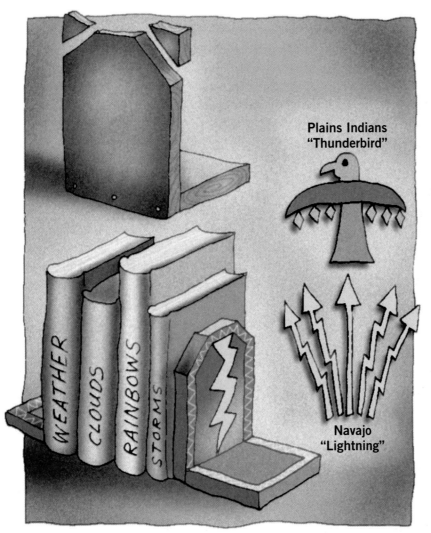

Plains Indians "Thunderbird"

Navajo "Lightning"

1. Mark and cut the board into four pieces. Make the uprights slightly longer than the horizontal base pieces. Cut the corners diagonally on one end of each of the uprights.

2. Butting a base piece up against an upright, nail the wood together with three nails, evenly spaced. Repeat for the other bookend.

3. Sand the edges and any rough spots on the wood smooth. Paint the bookends, using one of the designs shown here, or inventing your own. (Remember that the long, flat side of the bookends will not show; that side pushes against the books. Do your artwork on the other side.)

Index
To Activity Sections

More Good Children's Books from
Williamson Publishing

PARENTS' CHOICE HONOR AWARD WINNER!
STEPPING STONES MULTICULTURAL HONOR AWARD!
BENJAMIN FRANKLIN BEST JUVENILE FICTION AWARD!

TALES ALIVE!
Ten Multicultural Folktales with Activities
   by Susan Milord
   128 pages, full-color paintings and illustrations
   Trade paper, $15.95

The following **Kids Can!** books for ages 4 to 10 are each 160-178 pages, fully illustrated, trade paper, 11 x 8 ½, $12.95 US.

HANDS AROUND THE WORLD
365 Creative Ways to Build Cultural
   Awareness & Global Respect
   by Susan Milord

PARENTS' CHOICE GOLD AWARD WINNER!
PARENTS MAGAZINE PARENTS' PICK!

THE KIDS' NATURE BOOK
365 Indoor/Outdoor Activities and Experiences/Revised Edition
   by Susan Milord

AMERICAN BOOKSELLER PICK OF THE LISTS

ADVENTURES IN ART
Art & Craft Experiences for 7- to 14-Year-Olds
   by Susan Milord

KIDS GARDEN!
The Anytime, Anyplace Guide to Sowing & Growing Fun
   by Avery Hart and Paul Mantell

SUPER SCIENCE CONCOCTIONS
50 Mysterious Mixtures for Fabulous Fun
   by Jill F. Hauser

THE KIDS' MULTICULTURAL COOKBOOK
Food & Fun Around the World
   by Deanna F. Cook

KIDS' COMPUTER CREATIONS
Using Your Computer for Art & Craft Fun
   by Carol Sabbeth

WINNER OF THE OPPENHEIM TOY PORTFOLIO BEST BOOK AWARD!
AMERICAN BOOKSELLER PICK OF THE LISTS

THE KIDS' SCIENCE BOOK
Creative Experiences for Hands-On Fun
   by Robert Hirschfeld and Nancy White

PARENTS' CHOICE GOLD AWARD WINNER!
AMERICAN BOOKSELLER PICK OF THE LISTS

THE KIDS' MULTICULTURAL ART BOOK
Art & Craft Experiences from Around the World
   by Alexandra M. Terzian

KIDS COOK!
Fabulous Food for the Whole Family
   by Sarah Williamson and Zachary Williamson

PARENTS' CHOICE GOLD AWARD WINNER!
BENJAMIN FRANKLIN BEST JUVENILE NONFICTION AWARD WINNER!

KIDS MAKE MUSIC!
Clapping and Tapping from Bach to Rock
   by Avery Hart and Paul Mantell

KIDS & WEEKENDS!
Creative Ways to Make Special Days
   by Avery Hart and Paul Mantell

WINNER OF THE OPPENHEIM TOY PORTFOLIO BEST BOOK AWARD!
SKIPPING STONES NATURE & ECOLOGY HONOR AWARD WINNER!

EcoArt!
Earth-Friendly Art & Craft Experiences for 3- to 9-Year-Olds
   by Laurie Carlson

AMERICAN BOOKSELLER PICK OF THE LISTS

KIDS' CRAZY CONCOCTIONS
50 Mysterious Mixtures for Art & Craft Fun
   by Jill Frankel Hauser

Additional copies of **Tales of the Shimmering Sky** and Williamson Publishing's award-winning **Kids Can!** books are available from your favorite bookseller or directly from:

WILLIAMSON PUBLISHING CO.
P.O. BOX 185
CHARLOTTE, VERMONT 05445,

Please add $3.00 for postage for one book plus 50 cents for each additional book. Or call toll-free with credit cards: **1-800-234-8791**. Satisfaction is guaranteed or full refund without questions or quibbles. Thank you.

Prices may be slightly higher when purchased in Canada.